LOVING
THE
HEAD MAN

Katherine
Cachitorie

AUSTIN BROOK PUBLISHING
America's stomping ground for romantic books.

This novel is a work of fiction. All characters are fictitious. Any similarities to anyone living or dead are completely accidental. The specific mention of known places or venues are not meant to be exact replicas of those places, but are purposely embellished or imagined for the story's sake.

ISBN:0615563686
ISBN-13:978-0615563688

INTERRACIAL ROMANCE
FROM
BESTSELLING AUTHOR

KATHERINE CACHITORIE:

SOME CAME DESPERATE: A LOVE SAGA

AND

WHEN WE GET MARRIED

ONE

Bree Hudson sat on the bed inside the fancy company condo reserved for clients, as Alan DeFrame showered, as he prepared himself, in the adjacent bathroom. She knew what she was about to do was as low as she could go. She knew it was so outside of who she was as a person that she still couldn't believe she had agreed. She wasn't like those anything-for-my-career females, she'd never dream of sleeping her way to the top. She hated even the idea of doing something that vile.

But here she was, stark naked in this little used, sterile bedroom, waiting for her supervisor to get out of the shower and pump on her as if he was pumping a piece of iron, and vile couldn't describe how awful she felt. Her father, if he could see her now, would be turning in his grave. He would have declared that nothing, not a solitary thing, should have reduced her to this.

There were reasons, of course. She could cite them chapter and verse. Powerfully good reasons, if you asked Bree. From Alan refusing to give her that job appointment and bonus check that she rightfully earned unless she consented to sleep with him, to her irresponsible mother putting the family home at risk and creating a monumental crisis at the worst possible time. She had powerful reasons. But that still didn't negate the fact that she was about to prostitute herself. And that still didn't stop her from hearing her father's voice echoing in her ear like a warning ghost: "Never do anything, baby girl," he once said to her, his voice by then a mere whisper, "that requires your self-respect for payment."

Bree closed her eyes and fought back tears as she sat on that bed. He was a proud man, her father, who died before she graduated law school, before he could see the fruits of his lifelong hard labor. On his dying bed he made her promise to take care of their impoverished family, to get all five of her younger siblings through college too, a role he had every intention of fulfilling himself before cancer struck him down.

He also made her promise to take care of her mother, who was much younger than her father and as wild and irresponsible as they come. It wasn't fair, her father had told her, she didn't deserve such a burden. But she was the only human being on the face of this earth that he knew he could depend on.

And now here she was, her father's daughter, allowing herself to be treated like some whore, knowing that the promise she was buying would require a part of her essence, of her very being, as payment. Alan worked directly for the head man, for Robert Colgate himself, and had dangled his power and position in front of her, with his unsavory offer, at a time when his refusal to be fair and her own family crisis had given her no choice, no choice at all, but to snatch that offer.

But as soon as the shower was turned off, and she could hear Alan stepping out of the stall, she knew she couldn't do it. She couldn't defame her father's good name, or toss away her own self-respect, like this. Her family was in a bad way, and needed her to get that bonus check unlike she'd ever needed to get anything before. But she couldn't do it, not like *this*. She just couldn't!

She got off of that bed, grabbed her clothes that were lying on a chair, and ran out of the bedroom. Her plan was to dress up front and then get the hell out of there, all before Alan came out of the bathroom. But as soon as she entered the living room, and before she could even slip into her panties, the door to the company's condo was unlocked and opened, and Robert Colgate himself, the head man himself, walked in.

He was a big man, tall and muscular, a man who commanded every room he entered, and Bree could hardly believe that he had just entered

9

this one. Her luck, she thought, couldn't possibly be this bad.

Robert, however, was in shock for a different reason. He could hardly believe what he was seeing, as his large, violet-blue eyes stared in stunned confusion as Brianna Hudson stood before him naked as a newborn babe. A babe, that is, with a fine, ripe, sultry black body that caused his manhood to throb as soon as he laid eyes on her. He had been out of town on the highest-profiled case of his career, and hadn't had a chance to get in touch with his office here in Chicago, but he hadn't been away that long! And what was she doing here, in the company's condo, anyway? She didn't have this level of clearance!

"*Brianna*?" he asked, unable to hide his confusion, his surprise.

But the shock was yet to come when Alan DeFrame, his trusted lieutenant and the man who ran the program Bree was competing in, came out of the bedroom stark-naked and freshly showered, calling her name.

Just three months ago a scene like that would have been unthinkable. Brianna Shakira Hudson had arrived at the mammoth Colgate office building in downtown Chicago ready to set the world on fire. She just stood there smiling that day, in the middle of the massive lobby of marble and glass, in her best business suit and slim-line briefcase, as thongs of other business suits and briefcases hurried past her in the hustle and bustle that reeked of life in the big time.

She could hardly believe her good luck. A girl like her on a stage like this. Her late father, who used to be a hard-working Mississippi janitor who never made it beyond the eighth grade, would have grinned from ear to ear if he would have lived to see a day like this.

Nothing was guaranteed to her, however. She was only one of ten finalists selected from newly-graduated law students across the country to compete in a twelve-week program at the illustrious Colgate and Associates law firm. Only one finalist would be offered a coveted position and the guaranteed fifty-thousand dollar bonus check at the end of the program. Which meant the other nine finalists would leave with nothing but the privilege of saying in future job interviews, or on resumes, that they had participated in one of the most prestigious, most sought-after training programs in the world.

But Bree was certain that she would be the one hired by Colgate at the program's end. She was certain that no-one needed it more than she did or was willing to work harder to get it. This was the chance of a lifetime for her. Not just because of the potential job offer itself and the signing bonus, which were huge. But mainly because she would be at the top of her profession. She'd be working at a prestigious firm like Colgate that would more than afford her the means to fulfill her promise to her father, the promise to take care of her family back home, her impoverished, always-got-drama-going-on family, and she was more than ready to give it her all.

To her dismay, however, it didn't start out as promising as she had hoped. Especially when she met Alan DeFrame.

She was the seventh finalist to go in for the meet and greet with the program's supervisor. The other six finalists had returned looking harried and terrified, it seemed to Bree, but then they'd laugh it off as if they had misunderstood what had really taken place.

"There will be blood," number four had jokingly said.

"It will be brutal," number six had smiled and commented.

And then it was Bree's turn.

Alan DeFrame sat behind the large desk in his large office flipping through stacks of documents as if he were searching almost frantically for something. He was also on his cell phone, explaining to his caller that he thought he had the document in front of him. His face was frowned and his look completely concentrated on the task at hand. He didn't so much as acknowledge Bree, or even realize she was standing in front of his desk, until he had ended his cell phone call and bothered to look up.

He was easily handsome, Bree thought, with the sharp, angular features of a male model: thin but muscular physique, high cheek bones, a long nose, attractively puckered lips. His hair was a strawberry blonde and his eyes were a kind of murky blue. With his good looks and those stylish prescription glasses on his face, he came across as both snarky and sexy. He would have been remarkably attractive in fact, Bree thought, if he didn't give off the air of somebody who knew he looked good and not only loved the fact, but flaunted it.

"Which one are you?" he asked her, unabashedly looking up and then down her entire body. Not bad, he thought as he checked her out. About five-five or so in height, long, neatly braided hair framing her small, cute face, almond-shaped bright brown eyes, full lips. Although she was a little darker and more ethnic-looking than he usually found attractive, and wasn't razor-thin the way he liked his females to be, her curves were in all the right places and worked beautifully on her. Yes, he thought again. He will definitely like a piece of that.

"Say again?" he asked her when his preoccupation caused him to miss what she had said.

"Hudson," Bree said. "I said my name is Bree Hudson."

"Yes, that's right," he said as he began searching through a different pile of files on his messy desk. When he found the one he was looking for, he opened it and began reading from it. "Brianna Shakira Hudson. Mississippi Coastal Law School. Graduated high in your class, but not the highest. Was the vice-president of various organizations, but never president. Was on the law review, but was not its editor." He looked up again. "Are these facts accurate?"

"Yes, sir, I was—"

"Not what one would call a glowing curriculum vitae, wouldn't you agree?" He tossed her folder aside.

Bree stared at him. "I'm pleased with what I've done, sir."

"Pleased?"

"Yes, sir," Bree replied confidently. "I think my college career was exemplary, especially when you consider that I was the first person in my family to ever go to—"

"Sit down," he said, interrupting her.

Bree just stood there, unable to quite understand.

"Sit down, I said," Alan ordered. "Oh, come now, Miss Hudson. You've got to be a lot faster on your feet than that if you expect to make it here at Colgate."

Bree felt as if she had walked into an exam she didn't know she was having, and had turned up completely unprepared. She sat down in the chair in front of Alan's desk. He was now searching again through the various papers on his desk.

"You were early this morning," he said.

"Yes, sir," Bree said, thrilled that someone had told him that she was the first to arrive. "Where I come from they say the early bird catches the worms."

"Be on time next time," he said without looking up. "Not too early. Not late. On time." He looked at her over the top tip of his glasses. "There are no worms to be caught here. Understood?"

Bree nodded, confused. "Yes, sir," she said, unable to hide her growing disappointment.

He stopped searching through his papers and considered her. Then he tossed his glasses on his already overcrowded desk, ran his hand through his hair, and leaned back. "I'm a blunt man, Miss Hudson. That's why Mr. Colgate put me in charge of his recruitment program. He knows I won't b/s him. He asks my opinion, I give it to him straight. Do you find that quality admirable, Miss Hudson?"

"Bluntness? Absolutely."

"Why?"

There was probably no right answer, Bree was beginning to believe, but she plowed ahead anyway. "Because the truth is always preferable."

"Even if it hurts?"

"Especially if it hurts."

"Here's some truth then," Alan said, leaning forward, his blue eyes blazing. "You don't stand a rat's chance in hell to make it here at Colgate."

Bree felt as if her heart had momentarily stopped. He wasn't joking, either. He wasn't cracking one smile. And she immediately felt defensive, batting her large eyes as she was prone to do whenever she felt under siege. "May I ask why you believe so?"

"Because you've never been at the top of anything. You've been close, but never at the top. The bridesmaid, never the bride? We have over three hundred attorneys working at Colgate. Three hundred. And every one of them, me included, was number one. All of the other finalists, all nine of them, graduated head of their classes, too. Every one of them. Not second, not third, the head. Except you. And you're some poor nobody from some nothing Mississippi law school and you still weren't number one? Give me a break! It's a fluke you're even here, Miss Hudson, a shot in the dark. And flukes and shots in the dark rarely make it anywhere. Especially at a top firm like this one." Then he leaned back again. "How's that for truth?"

Bree felt crestfallen, but she wasn't about to let him know it. "Colgate has a rigorous selection process. The fact that I was selected—"

"Doesn't mean a damn thing." Then he paused, considered her again. "You want to know why you were selected?" he asked her. "You really want to know?"

She wasn't sure if she did or not at this point, but she nodded anyway. "Yes, that would be helpful," she said, batting her eyes again.

Alan smiled at the cute way she batted her eyes. But then he turned serious. "The boss happened to walk into the board room at the time that we, the selection committee, were reviewing applicant videos, the ones where you guys sat before a camera and told us about your legal philosophy. Your video happened to be on the screen when he entered the room, and he stopped and watched it. It could have been anybody else's video at that moment in time, but as fate would have it, it was yours."

He paused again, as if remembering the oddness of it. "And the boss didn't say a word about it," Alan continued, "didn't let on that he was even impressed. He just ordered us to do whatever it was he had come into the room to order us to do, and left. Some days later, when I gave him the names of the ten finalists who had made the cut, he told me to re-cut and include you."

He looked at Bree as if he resented her. "That's how you made it here, Miss Hudson," he said. "You happened to light up the screen at the same time Robert Colgate happened to enter the room. And he apparently liked what he saw or what he heard or whatever. That's why you're here. You weren't selected, certainly not by me or the committee I chair. You're here because Robert Colgate, the head man himself, threw you a lifeline. But he's a hard man; don't be seduced by his graciousness. He may throw that lifeline your way, but it's up to you to grab it and swim. Which is probably where you'll fail miserably. In the swimming. Now," Alan said with a grin, "was that helpful enough?"

Bree didn't know what to say. All of her fight seemed to want to seep out of her. Why was everything such a battle for her? She stammered. "I don't . . . I mean—"

And Alan pounced. "Come now," he said, "is that the best you can do, Miss Hudson? I just told you some searing truth. You don't belong here. You took somebody else's spot. And all you can say is *you don't*?"

"I mean, I didn't realize—"

"You didn't realize? What the devil does your realization have to do with this? I'm talking about your future here. I'm talking about your chance of making it all the way to the top of your profession. And you didn't realize?"

Bree was determined to keep it together. "I'm grateful that Mr. Colgate—"

"He doesn't want your gratitude. Who the hell are you? Ah, you're pathetic!"

And it continued that way for a good long time. The other finalist was right: it was brutal. Every answer Bree gave made her feel more and more inadequate. Alan DeFrame's brilliance allowed him to toy with her, to take what should have been seen as virtuous about her, like her humble beginnings, like her hard work and determination, and turn it inside out.

She knew he was testing her. She knew he was baptizing her in the fire of the big leagues. He wanted to know if she could take it, if she could handle the heat. And she knew she could. That was why she allowed him to castigate her, to brutalize her just as the others had said he would. But her willingness changed when Alan walked around to the front of his desk, and told her to stand up.

It seemed an odd request, but nothing about her meet and greet with Alan DeFrame could be classified as ordinary. Stand up, he said, so she stood up. But when he began slowly appraising her, looking her up and down as if he was inspecting a model for his runway, not an attorney for his law firm, she began to get concerned.

"Remove that jacket so I can get a look at you," he ordered.

She did that, too, revealing a soft white, sleeveless blouse tucked into a tight black skirt. She was curvaceous and seemed to have it together, although she rarely worked out.

He removed the jacket from her arm and tossed it onto the chair. "Turn around," he again ordered, and she did that too, although she still didn't see the reason for such an inspection. She knew she was no fashion plate, if that was his point. She'd had too many financial obligations to her younger siblings, to her irresponsible mother, to her trifling older brother Ricky to ever have enough money to give in to vanities. That was why her business suit was off the rack department store, rather than the tailored looks favored by the Colgate crowd.

She expected Alan to rip into her appearance when he told her to turn around, and to make some comment about how his grandmother had more style. But he didn't say a word. When she was about to turn back around, however, he had moved up behind her and placed his hands on her hips. She immediately protested, moving quickly and angrily to turn, but he tightened his grip and pulled her closer against him, rendering her immobile.

"What do you think you're doing?" he asked her in a soft, but undeniably stern voice.

It was more of a question Bree figured she should have been asking, given what he was doing to *her*, but she said, instead, "please let me go," in her own brand of sternness.

"And what if I don't?" he quickly replied In a snarky tone. "What are you going to do about it? Scream? Cry foul? Take your marbles and go home? Because that's where you'll be going, Miss Hudson, if you even think about disrespecting me."

Disrespecting him? she thought. *Was this guy nuts*? "I'm not disrespecting you, Mr. DeFrame," she said. "Just please let me go. Just take your hands off of me now." She said this with finality, as if it was her last warning, but Alan seemed to relish the challenge.

"I'll take my hands off of you when I'm good and ready to take my hands off of you." He began massaging her hips, holding her tighter still. Bree cringed and angrily tried to move out of his grasp again, but again his grip tightened and she couldn't take one step. She could feel him expanding against her, as if an interview she thought would be all about business, had disintegrated into a sex romp for him.

"You got what it takes, you know that, Bree?" His mouth was within a half inch of her ear. She could feel his hot breath. His eyes were assessing her smooth, thin, swan-like neck. "Of all the others, you got it, baby. That's why Mr. Colgate told me to bump somebody more deserving and give the last slot to you. He saw something in you, too. He mentioned something about trial presence. He believes you have what it takes to win over a wavering jury, to get that favorable outcome, which he views as priceless in our line of work. But I'm not Robert Colgate. I don't give a damn who you win over. When I look at you, I don't see any skills of persuasion, or courtroom presence. When I look at you, I see skills in the bedroom. I see you naked beneath me, this fine ass of yours—"

"Let me go!" Bree said as forcefully as she knew how, trying with all she had to sling herself away from him, literally tussling with him to get away. "I'm not playing now," she warned, her teeth clenched. "Let me go!"

Her indignation seemed to anger him, instead of shame him, and he slammed her harder against him, encircling her with one hand and grabbing her by the chin with the other. At first it was a battle, as she fought hard against his pull. But he was far too strong. He managed to turn her head sideways and her chin upwards, until she was stubbornly looking him in his face.

"Who do you think you're talking to like that?" he said to her. She was even cuter, he thought, when she was angry. "You think I'm one of those country boys back home? Are you foolish enough to believe that? You're ambitious or your black ass wouldn't be here, so let's cut the good girl routine, all right? You want what I've got because I'm the man who stands between you and your greatest dream, girl, you'd better remember who you're talking to!"

He exhaled, regret showing in his murky blue eyes. "I was just trying to help you out. I was trying to give you a leg up since your limited abilities certainly aren't going to do you any favors. You're competing against the cream of the crop, woman. The best of the best. And you come here from some backward Mississippi watering hole with some second rate education and expect to be in contention for a job at *Colgate*? Are you *kidding* me?"

Again he paused, again Bree battled to be free. But he kept on talking. "You're cute, but you aren't all that. Almost every female out there better looking than you. But Colgate saw something in you, something that made him question our selections, something he'd never done in all the years I'd been running this program. So I figure hey, a ladies man like Robert Colgate sees something in you, there has to be something there. It can't be your looks; I don't see anything remarkable about that face. You're just another cute face, if you ask me. So it must be this fine body of yours." He pulled her closer still; Bree fought him even harder still.

"What's wrong with you?" he asked angrily, ramming her against him, seemingly amazed by her willingly to battle him back. "All those other female finalists out there know how to play the game, they didn't give me this hard a time, and every one of them already stands a better chance than you. What's your damn problem?"

Yet another pause, still more regret in his eyes. "Thought I'd let you prove to me that you've got more going for you than your background, because that's going against you. But you want to play the innocent. You want to play the virtuous woman who wouldn't dream of sleeping her way to the top. Then fine. Play her. But when you're ready to play it my way, which you will when reality sets in, come see me."

Then he not only released her, but shoved her away from him as if she disgusted him now. She stumbled and turned around quickly, mortified by his treatment. She raked her hand through her braids, raking them out of her face, and stared at Alan DeFrame in disbelief. Tears strained her lids.

"Get out of my sight," he ordered in a nasty tone. "Consider this meet and greet a failure." And then he turned and walked back behind his desk.

Bree stood there momentarily, stunned, dumbstruck, angry and sad, more emotions building inside of her than she could even express, and then she did as he ordered, and got out of his sight.

And like her colleagues, she left his office in a daze. But as soon as she saw the other finalists, she couldn't laugh it off the way they had, she couldn't call it brutal as if his brutality was all in the game. She, instead, got away from them, too. Alan's behavior was a joke to them, something up-and-comers had to simply endure. But his sex-laden harshness wasn't funny to Bree, and she wasn't interested in *enduring* it.

That was why she kept walking. Out of Alan's office, out of the board room where the other finalists were assembled, across the hall and into the stairwell. She went up the stairs to the roof deck where Monty Ross, Mr. Colgate's assistant, had showed them when he gave them a tour of the building earlier that morning. Monty had called it a haven, the place to go if you wanted to get outside to smoke or to gather your thoughts or just to get away, without going all the way downstairs.

For Bree, it was a getaway. A place not only to gather her thoughts, but to decide if she should report Alan DeFrame's ass to the EEOC or just get back on the bus for Mississippi now. Toss her dream to the wolves since they were already trying to devour it.

She opened the stubborn door of that roof top and walked to its' rail, inhaling the windy March breeze and taking in a top-side view of the great Chicago skyline.

She didn't realize it, because she didn't bother to look, but she had company on that roof. For Robert Colgate was seated beside a table near the back, his legs casually crossed in an elegant pose, as he sipped his coffee, smoked his cigarette, and stared in surprised silence as the same young woman who had been haunting his dreams, suddenly appeared.

TWO

Bree didn't realize Robert Colgate was staring, she had no clue that anyone else was on that rooftop, because her entire concentration was on that encounter she had just endured with Alan DeFrame. She stood at the rail, her braids blowing in the wind, and she had to fight with all she had to keep from breaking down in tears. Alan made it sound as if she would never be victorious unless she gave in to his perverted whims, which she was certain she would never do. But if she didn't, he'd made even clearer, she may as well pack up and leave now because she didn't stand a chance.

She wiped a tear that had escaped from her eye. Because she knew she couldn't pack up and leave. She had too much riding on a successful outcome. She couldn't sit back and let a jerk like Alan DeFrame determine her destiny or, even worst, her family's destiny.

She, instead, stared out over that rail and considered her options. She could turn him in, of course, to the firm's HR Department, or even to the EEOC. But how could she prove her allegations? Although he had pressed against her and touched her inappropriately, and his words made clear that she had better get with the program or else, she still would have to prove it.

And the other finalists certainly weren't going to back her up. They all laughed it off when they came out of Alan's office, even though they admitted the encounter was brutal. Bree was convinced that if she accused a man like him of bad behavior, she'd be on her own, and would more likely be the one chastised and blamed. She may even be asked to leave the program. Maybe even sued for defamation of character by the brilliant attorney DeFrame. He seemed like the type.

Bree sighed in a loud, anguished release. She would have to give it time, think her options through carefully, before she made any moves.

Just as she made up her mind to wait, her cell phone began ringing. She looked at the Caller ID. It was her mother.

"Ricky's in jail," her mother said into the phone as soon as Bree said hello. Fannie Hudson wasn't predictable when it came to most matters, except when it came to her devotion to Bree's sorry older brother.

"He's in jail again?" Bree asked. "He just got out." She had the phone on speaker, because her mother tended to yell rather than talk. And because of that Robert, who had no intentions of overhearing her private conversation, heard every word.

"It's bad this time, Brianna," her mother said into the phone. "Don't you minimize this."

"I'm not minimizing anything."

27

"He's the best child I have and you don't like it so you're always bad-mouthing him."

Bree rolled her eyes. Her mother spoke of Ricky as if he was a wonderful, delicate soul, not the lazy, selfish, trifling thug he was. "What did he do this time?" she decided to ask, refusing to get into it with her mother.

"It's bad, baby girl. It's bad."

Her mother began crying. Bree folded one arm and closed her eyes. What she would give to have this monkey of responsibility off her back. Her mother, who ran the streets worse than a teenager did, always out partying with Ricky and his friends, getting drunk, smoking weed, sleeping around with every Tom, Dick, and Harry even while Bree's father was on his dying bed. And Bree's five younger siblings, the oldest fifteen, the youngest eight, were the ones who would suffer in the end. "Just tell me what he's done this time," she tried to say patiently, although her bitterness shone through.

"They say he jumped on Keisha, his baby mama. But you know Ricky wouldn't jump on a girl. She just lying because he wouldn't let her dump them kids on him so she can party with her friends and hang out with her new man. So now she wanna claim he beat her."

"Okay, well, you weren't there and neither were I," Bree said, "so we can't say what he did or didn't do."

"I can say it!" her mother shot back, causing her voice to ring out even louder over the speaker. "Don't you dare tell me what I can't say. That's my child and those racist police ain't taking him away from me again. Not again!" And the crying started up again.

"Ma, I've got to go," Bree said, long ready to end this painful call. "There's nothing I can do about it, anyway. Ricky gets himself into these stupid situations, he's the one who has to get himself out of them. There's nothing I can do."

"Ain't nothing you can do?" her mother yelled. "There's plenty you can do!"

Bree frowned. "Like what?"

"You're a lawyer, ain't you? You just graduated law school, didn't you? Get your ass back here to Mississippi and help your brother!"

"Ma, you know I can't leave right now. I just got here."

"So when you coming home?"

"The program ends by Memorial Day--"

"*Memorial Day*? You done lost your mind! That ain't 'till the end of May! He'll be rotting in prison by Memorial Day!"

"Well that's the only time I won't have to be here and I'm not about to lose this opportunity over Ricky's foolishness." *If I haven't lost it already*, Bree thought.

"Yeah, I told him you didn't give a damn," her mother declared. "I told him I would be wasting my time calling you. Because it's always all about you. Forget your family. Forget your big brother. Forget the promise you made to your poor old daddy."

This hurt Bree to her core, as she was certain her mother knew it would. "I'm keeping my promise to Daddy. That's why I'm here. If I can make it, then I can help y'all."

"Ain't stuttin' us," her mother went on. "Just living it up in the big city, in *Chicago*, like you the big time girl now. When poor Ricky sittin' in that filthy jail cell—"

"Ma, I have to go," Bree said. "I'll call you later."

And she clicked off her cell. She hated doing that to her mother, and she hated that her brother was in trouble again, but what did they expect her to do about it? Leave everything behind and come running to help a brother who was always in and out of jail?

She shook her head as if she could shake away the thought of it. She was determined to be the one selected to work at Colgate, despite Alan DeFrame, despite her fierce competition, despite her mother's badgering to make sure her time away from home wasn't about to be carefree. As if she'd ever had a carefree day in her entire life.

"Aren't you cold?" a male's voice said from behind her and Bree, startled, turned to the sound.

And that was when she realized that she was not alone. To the right of the roof's door, seated relaxed at a table, was a man she immediately recognized as Robert Colgate, the owner of the firm she was desperately trying to become a member of, and one of the most renowned criminal defense attorneys in the country. She could hardly believe her eyes.

She was caught so off guard, in fact, that her first reaction wasn't just amazement over the fact that Robert Colgate had just spoken to her, but shock that he may have overheard the extremely personal, *bare* conversation she had just had with her mother.

"Am I . . . cold?" she found herself asking.

Robert lifted his eyebrows, his very pronounced, perfect eyebrows, Bree noticed. He was seated beside a small, oval table, legs crossed, drinking coffee and smoking a cigarette. "I believe that was my question, yes," he said.

She looked younger than her video, more vibrant, but Robert still saw that sweetness in her, that *something special* that made him order Alan DeFrame to reshuffle the committee selections, and include her.

When Bree still seemed at a loss for words, he smiled. "Come here," he said.

Bree moved over without hesitation. She knew who he was and just to be able to speak with him made her excited beyond words. Should she joke off the phone call she had just had, noting that her mother was always "kidding around?" Should she tell him what had just transpired with Alan DeFrame? Was he the kind of man who wouldn't tolerate such behavior? Or was he just as bad? Bree had so many questions, so many concerns, that she didn't know where to begin.

Robert looked at her white, sleeveless blouse, a blouse that had a low-cut, looped down collar, with his expression unreadable to Bree. "What I was trying to say is that it's rather cool to be standing out here in a sleeveless blouse." He looked down at her sizeable breasts. "No matter how attractive the view."

Bree felt her face flush when he looked back up at her. His eyes were a soft, violet blue, but had an intensity within them that unnerved her. "I'm fine," she said, rubbing her bare arm, realizing for the first time that she had left her jacket in Alan's office. "I never really get cold."

"That's because you're still very young. Keep living. You'll cover up." Then he stood to his feet. "Come here," he said.

He began taking off his suit coat as she walked up to him, that earnest, wide-eyed look he remembered from her video piercing her face now. When he first walked into that board room and saw her on that screen, and looked into those big, sincere eyes of hers that dominated the screen, a strong, almost paternalistic sensation came over him. He shielded his feelings, years of courtroom experience had made him a master at that, but he had never experienced such a reaction like that before.

The selection process required that each applicant send a video explaining their overall legal philosophy. And there was Bree, sitting on a stool and simply telling what she thought. She was so naïve, Robert had thought as he had watched her; she had no clue how impractical her philosophy would be to live by. But that innocence, that sweetness, showed through like a burst of blinding light. And he felt seared by it. He felt as if he was seeing something so beautiful, so special, that he almost became emotional. And days later, when Alan DeFrame presented the list of the ten finalists for his ultimate approval, he told him to reconfigure, and include Brianna.

Now as she stood before him, he wrapped his expensive suit coat around her small body. He loved that sweet, fresh, scent of her, loved the way her braids bounced in the wind, loved the way her bright brown eyes looked up at him, as if she was anticipating something great to come from him, as if she admired him.

"That better?" he asked her in a soft tone, unable to stop pulling the coat lapels together, effective holding her by the catch of those lapels, unable to release her from his grasp.

"Yes, sir, it's much better. Thank-you."

He continued to stare into her eyes. Bree felt strange this close to him, almost heady. "You're okay?" he asked her.

"Yes," she said in an almost breathless tone. This was too close. She was uncomfortable this close.

Robert saw her discomfort and felt embarrassed, almost angry that he was behaving so oddly toward her, that a woman he didn't even know could have such a pull on his emotions. He released her, but couldn't let her leave just yet. "Have a seat," he said.

Bree sat down, gladly. She didn't feel as uneasy when she sat down, especially if she considered the scene. Here she was, a poor girl from Mississippi, sitting with one of the richest, most famous attorneys in America. And even with that fact in mind she hadn't turned into some babbling idiot. She was pleased with herself.

Robert sat down too. It was a turn-on for him to see his suit coat wrapped around her voluptuously appealing body. "What brings you up here, Brianna?" he asked her.

She was surprised that he knew her name. Thought about mentioning Alan's boorish behavior, then thought again. Although it wasn't fair, she knew that any wrong word could send her packing. "I needed to take a break. Monty Ross said this was a great hideaway."

"It is. That's why I'm up here." Robert said this with a smile. Bree loved the way those lines of age and experience appeared on the side of his eyes. "But this is your first day. What could you possibly be hiding away from so soon?"

Bree decided to test him. He seemed reasonable when she used to watch him on TV, where he often appeared as a legal analyst on CNN, MSNBC, and sometimes Fox. "We had our meet and greet with Mr. DeFrame this morning." She said this and then looked intensely at Robert, to gauge his reaction.

"Ah," he said with a knowing nod, as if he understood, and Bree waited for more. But he had nothing more to say.

She decided to leave it alone. This moment was too rare. She had an audience with the head of the firm, the undisputed boss. She wanted to stay focused. Besides, his coat felt so warm against her skin, and smelled so cologne-fresh and clean that she found herself snuggling further into it. She wasn't messing up this wonderful moment. "I'm surprised you recognize me as one of the finalist," she said with a smile, remembering how Alan had said that Robert Colgate hand-picked her, hoping to get further insight as to why.

"Nothing surprising about it," Robert said. "I make it my business to be aware of all of the people interested in working for me."

She decided to go there. "But it'll be Alan DeFrame who makes the final decision on who gets that one position. Right?"

Bree was looking at Robert so forlornly that he felt the need to reassure her. "Alan recommends," he said, "but I make the final decision."

"So you'll decide who gets the position?" She said this too excitedly.

Robert didn't see the need to repeat what he had already made clear. He, instead, pulled out his ever-chirping smartphone and began reviewing a text message.

Bree found herself staring at Robert. Although he looked less intense now than he did on those cable news shows he often frequented, he looked far more attractive in person. He had such a handsome, earnest-looking face, with a head full of light-brown hair, unblemished tanned skin, even darker eyebrows above those soft violet eyes that seemed trusting and suspicious all at the same time.

His body was impressive too, as he had a muscular and elegant physique, but Bree was drawn to his face. To his strong, wide jaw, to his intense, intelligent gaze, to the fact that the papers said he was thirty-eight, but at some angles he didn't look a day over thirty. Before she knew it, she blurted out, "You're Robert Colgate."

She was horrified as soon as she realized what she had done. She almost sounded like some countrified groupie. To her relief, however, it didn't seem to bother him at all. He even smiled a wonderful smile, but he didn't look up. He seemed distracted by his text message.

"And you're Brianna Hudson," he said back to her.

"I'm still surprised that you know my name."

"You know mine."

"Yeah, but you're . . . Robert Colgate. I'm supposed to know your name."

He placed his smartphone on the table and looked at her. "You're a finalist for a position at my firm. I'm supposed to know yours."

Bree had read about how committed he was to his law firm and refused to be the absent owner. She looked at his cigarette. None of the articles she'd ever read about him, and she'd read many, mentioned that he smoked, however.

When he saw that she was staring at the cigarette between his fingers, he snorted lightly, and began dousing it out, uncrossing his leg and turning his body toward the table as he did. Bree couldn't help but notice the muscles that strained the expensive fabric of his dress shirt. "One of my guilty pleasures," he said.

"I figure you'd to be too smart to do that to your body."

"You're right, of course, it's a terrible habit to have. But sometimes I have to indulge my lesser nature."

"Why?" she asked.

This question seemed to disturb Robert, it seemed to Bree, which surprised her. "Why?" he asked. "Because I'm a human being who sometimes need a stress reliever." He glanced down at her cleavage. He'd had dreams of this sweet brown beauty relieving his stress, wiggling beneath him as he pounded her. The mere thought of it now caused his manhood to thump against his boxers.

"I'm sure there's a lot on your plate," Bree said.

"The understatement of the year," he said with another smile, as if she had just spoken some serious truth, and only after he admitted it did Bree see the exhaustion on his face. "There's always a lot on my plate," he added.

Bree frowned. "But you're the boss with three hundred lawyers working for you. Why don't you farm out some of your cases?"

"Because our elite clients pay top dollar for the boss, not for the farmhand."

Bree smiled, understanding that. "Then maybe you should start turning down more work."

"I already turn down a lot of work." He looked at Bree and was pleased by her concern. "But thanks for the suggestions."

That face of hers haunted him. It wasn't just that it was a pretty face, pretty faces, to Robert, were a dime a dozen in the circles he traveled. But Bree had a unique look, something that made him feel warm and pleased, not the usual suspiciousness he often felt whenever a new person entered his orbit. And being around her made him feel as if he could actually be the good, caring man he used to be, instead of the sick, ruthless bastard he sometimes felt he'd become. Especially whenever he was at trial, defending all manner of perverted scum and, thanks to his renowned courtroom skills, always getting them off.

"You didn't turn down that rapper," Bree said, feeling oddly comfortable talking shop with the boss. "Doesn't his trial begin next week? What's his name? Jay-Pack or something?"

Robert looked as if he didn't want to be reminded of it. "Jay-Pat," he said. "Legally known as Jayson Patrick. And yes, his trial starts next Monday if all goes according to plan."

"Are you worried?"

"I'm always worried when I'm asked to defend someone against a murder charge."

"And in Los Angeles of all places. In Hollywood."

"Yep," Robert said, running his hand across his face, his exhaustion even more pronounced. "I'll be flying out there this weekend."

The idea of not being able to feast her eyes on this man anytime soon, depending on how long that trial lasts, depressed her. "If you believe the papers," she said, "he's guilty as sin."

Robert looked at her intensely. "You believe the papers?"

"I wouldn't say I believe them. I read them." Then she shook her head. "I could never be a criminal defense attorney."

"Yeah, you mentioned that in your video. Good for you."

Bree smiled. "Good for me? But you're the best criminal attorney around. Why in the world would you think it's not a good idea to become one?"

Robert didn't respond at first. He just sat there, his hands now clasp on the table in front of him. It seemed to Bree that he was remembering something very unpleasant. "I just finished a trial this morning," he said. "Verdict came in at exactly nine-fifty-two. A quiet, sensible young man, the son of a billionaire banker from right here in Chicago, was my client. He was alleged to have savagely beaten and raped a young woman. Ruined her life, by all accounts. And I was his defense attorney."

Bree nodded. She had heard of the case. "So the verdict was guilty?"

"The verdict was *not guilty*."

Bree stared at him, puzzled.

"I never said I wasn't a very good defense attorney," he added.

Bree laughed. "You should be celebrating. You did your best for your client and got him off. You should be pleased."

"Pleased?" Robert spat out. "I should be pleased that a rapist has walked scot free, thanks to my amazing courtroom skills?"

Bree was astonished. "But if you knew he was guilty, why did you prove his innocence?"

"I didn't prove anything. It's not my job to prove his innocence. It's the DA's job to prove his guilt. And they failed miserably." Then he added bitterly: "Sorry asses."

"Maybe they weren't sorry, Mr. Colgate. Maybe you were just too brilliant."

Robert sipped from his now cold coffee. It was obvious to Bree that he wasn't buying what she was selling. He sat his coffee cup back down. "When I saw you on that video you submitted, I was impressed."

This pleased Bree. "Really?"

Robert frowned. "Not by your legal philosophy, I saw a lot of practical problems with your philosophy." Then he looked into her eyes, her kind, pretty, bright-brown eyes, he thought. "But I was impressed with you. I thought, well good, here is a young lady with a strong moral compass. Someone whose inner core meant more to her than gaining a position. A young lady who takes to heart the Biblical admonition, the one about what should it prosper a man if he should gain the whole world, and lose his own soul. I wanted you here for that very reason." He looked at her. "Keep your values as strong, as unbendable as you displayed them on that video, Brianna. If you do, you'll sleep well at night."

Bree stared at him, taken aback by his intensity. "Do you sleep well at night, Mr. Colgate?"

Robert smiled a smile loaded with so much charm, but even more regret. "I haven't had a good night's sleep in years, not since the night before I tried my first case as a criminal defense attorney."

Bree didn't know what to say to that. On TV, in magazines, he seemed so self-assured, so on top of his game that no-way could he find anything about his work reprehensible. She tried to smile. "You're a remarkable man. You're the best at something you hate."

"I don't hate it. I love it." He hesitated. "That's the problem. I love the fact that I've never lost a case. I love it too much."

Bree thought about this. "If you love it, then what's there to hate about it?"

Robert smiled again, but this time it was more like a smirk. "I hate the fact that I love it."

It didn't make sense to Bree, and it made perfect sense to Bree. For a few moments neither one of them spoke. Then Bree sighed. "The worst part for me is how unfair it all is."

"It's not unfair. It's the law."

"You mean it's better that a hundred guilty men go free rather than one innocent man be imprisoned? I understand what that means. And

I know the burden of proof is always on the prosecution. But it still seems unfair to me. I mean, what if the perp has a great defense attorney like you who can manipulate every aspect of the evidence? He'll get away with murder. While some poor boy in Mississippi, with a sorry lawyer, will end up behind bars for life. It's just not fair."

Robert remembered that she was from Mississippi, that she was a southern girl. "Then you should go back to Mississippi," he said, "and defend all of those poor Mississippi boys and level the playing field."

Bree looked alarmed. She didn't mean to sound as if she was criticizing what he did. "I didn't mean to—"

"How do you rate your chances here at Colgate?" he said, interrupting her just as his smartphone chirped again. He picked it up and began reading another text message.

Her heart dropped. Was he underwhelmed by her too, just as Alan DeFrame had been? "I would rate my chances as excellent, sir." She decided to give it one more try. "Although Mr. DeFrame said I don't stand a chance."

Robert continued to read his text message, although a frown enveloped his face. "Do you believe you stand a chance?" he asked her.

"Oh, yes, sir. I believe I'll win it all. I intend to win it all."

"You're in it to win it," Robert said with a small smile as he sat his phone back on the table. "Don't worry about Alan," he said. "Just do your best."

"And if I do my best and he still doesn't recommend me?"

Robert studied her. "Are you asking me to guarantee an outcome, Miss Hudson?"

Bree smiled and looked away from Robert. At that moment she did kind of feel like a used car salesman overselling her wares. When she looked back at him, however, she was stunned to see that he was staring at her cleavage. His eyes immediately moved back up to her face, and they were now hooded, lustful eyes. She flushed so hot she thought she had suddenly entered a steam room.

"I wasn't trying to suggest that you guarantee an outcome," she finally answered him. "I was just hoping that you would guarantee a fair process."

"I'll get with Alan and assess how well each of you are performing over the next twelve weeks," Robert said. "I guarantee a fair process."

Bree winced as the door to the outside deck pushed open and two men she remembered Monty had introduced as Colgate attorneys, entered. When they saw Robert, they moved in his direction. Robert, knowing that they were there on business, looked at Bree.

"You'd better get back downstairs, Brianna," he said.

Bree quickly stood up, took off his coat, and handed it to him.

"And put something on your arms," he admonished her as he accepted his coat. "You aren't too young to get pneumonia."

"Yes, sir," she said. "And have a nice day." She left, walking steadily toward the hard-to-open door, sensing that all eyes were trained on her.

And they were. The attorneys coming Robert's way looked back at her as she fled. One looked at Robert with one of those *who's that* head gestures, but Robert didn't notice the gesture, or the man making it, because he was still staring at Bree.

THREE

The next day she arrived on the twenty-first floor at Colgate to find all of her competitors already present. They all stood in the board room parading around like peacocks. Bree was the only African-American in the group, which was nothing new to her. She was one of only a handful of blacks in the whole of her law school, and was therefore accustomed to standing out that way.

But ethnicity wasn't the great divider in this group. Class was. For they all stood around in their Prada shoes, Versace suits, Dior bags and jewels, and talked a talk that sounded almost foreign to Bree. She tried her best to join in the conversations, to at least act like she had some sophistication, but she was roundly outmatched. They all talked about their visits to the south of France, about their Harvard-Yale-Princeton educations, about their father the judge, or mother the CEO, or brother the presidential appointee.

Bree was from dirt-poor circumstances, whose father worked for years as a school janitor before he died, and whose mother had serious partying and responsibility issues. Her father earned far less in months than the modest expense check Colgate had given the finalists just to participate in their twelve-week program.

And when the other finalists asked and Bree told them that she had graduated, not from any Ivy League university, but from Mississippi Coastal Law School, they looked at her, looked her up and down in fact, and then dismissed her out of hand with their eyes, with their body language, with the way they resumed the talk that only people of their social class could appreciate.

And just like that, after only one question and one answer, Bree was relegated to the back of the bus. Was the odd girl out again. And that doubt that had plagued her all of her life, tried to insinuate itself upon her once more, tried to make it clear that she was way out of her league.

But she ignored that voice, and listened to her father's reassuring voice, instead.

They all eventually sat down, and while they continued talking, Bree listened and observed. Her stiffest competition would come from Deidra Dentry and Prudence Cameron, she'd decided, because they were the leaders of what Bree called the pretty Prada girls, the ones who had the total package: the great looks and the great intellect. And Deidra Dentry, with her long blonde hair and brightest blue eyes, presented herself as the prettiest and smartest of them all.

And although many would conclude that Bree could easily be classified as pretty too, although it would be more along the lines of *something about her* than pure attractiveness, she never saw herself that way. She wouldn't have a clue how to use any feminine wiles to get some man to bend to her will, while Deidra and Prudence behaved like they were born to bend men, born to seduce every one.

But Bree wasn't moved. Her brains and hard work had gotten her there, and her brains and hard work, rather than any feminine wiles, would lead her to victory.

Alan DeFrame, along with Mark Ellerbee, his tall, razor thin, blonde-haired assistant, entered the board room just as some of the finalists were arguing over the merits of the *Citizens United* Supreme Court decision. It was a tired fight, it seemed to Bree, but they were fighting it tooth and nail, until Alan and Mark walked in.

After answering a series of housekeeping questions and process questions, Alan announced that they would be going to meet the boss.

"The boss?" Prudence, one of the pretty Prada girls, asked excitedly. "You mean Robert Colgate? We're going to meet Robert Colgate?"

"That's right," Alan said as he stood, causing everybody to stand to their feet as well. "You will get to meet the head man himself. And remember this: We're like Vegas. What goes on in this program, stays in this program. Not even Mr. Colgate is privy to our conversations, and he has no problem with that. Understand?" They all nodded, or verbalized, their understanding. It was like a cult, it seemed to Bree. They wanted in, and would do whatever it took to get in.

Alan turned to Mark Ellerbee. "Call Hyacinth and find out where he is."

"I'm on it," Mark said, pulling out his cell phone, following behind a fast-walking Alan DeFrame, as all of the finalists followed, too.

He was in the executive dining room on the top floor of the Colgate building. Bree thought it ridiculous that all of them would march into a dining hall and interrupt the man's breakfast, but Alan had no qualms about it whatsoever. He led them through the dining hall and then into a private room within the hall, a room so exclusive that Alan wasn't even senior enough to dine. Near the back in that room, at a rather elongated table, was a solitary figure. His legs were crossed as he sipped coffee and stared out the window at a sweeping view of rainy Chicago, the morning paper opened before him. It was Robert Colgate.

Unlike yesterday, when Bree talked with him on the top deck, he seemed well rested and relaxed today. He was dressed in a plain brown suit, white shirt, brown tie, but it all fit his impressively built, tanned body as if it had been stitched on. Not an ounce of fat seemed to be on the man. Although Bree had spoken with him the day before, she was just as excited as everyone else to see him.

"Good morning, Robert," Alan said strongly as he and his contingent approached. Robert turned at the sound of Alan's voice and looked at the approaching mob for the first time, his facial expression almost completely unchanged to them, although he did change. For Bree was with them, and although he was trained to keep his emotions hidden, she was the real object of his interest.

All of the finalists, including Bree, smiled as if they were meeting their favorite rock star and were giddy about it. In law circles, and to all of the finalists, it didn't get any bigger than Robert Colgate.

Although Robert didn't smile back at them, his cool demeanor warmed them.

"Ah, the Vegas group," he said and they all laughed. "I feel surrounded," he added, folding his newspaper. They all laughed again. Like robots, it seemed to Bree. "Please, everybody sit."

Bree found it almost comical the way the pretty girls jockeyed for seats close to Robert. Even the guys seemed aggressive. Bree didn't bother, the man, she felt, was too smart to be conned that way, and therefore was the last to sit down, ending up the farthest away. If face time was the issue, she didn't see what their problem was since he had a clear view of all of them.

Of course, the pretty Prada girls easily outshined all others as their ability to sell themselves with all of their feminine wiles came across more impressively. Bree listened carefully as each one described to Mr. Colgate their Ivy League educations, their judge father or surgeon mother or titan of industry grandpa. Despite Monty Ross's warnings earlier against self-promotion, they were dizzily self-promoting. Bree could hardly believe how they continually dropped their own name, as if determined to etch it into Robert's brain. How they could believe a man of his worldly savvy would fall for such amateurish overkill, was beyond her. But they kept at it, over and over. Deidra Dentry must have said her name ten different times in one paragraph.

Bree studied Robert as he studied the talkers. His facial expression was extremely difficult to read. He paid close attention to each person speaking, and seemed polite about it, but she couldn't tell if he bought into their hype, or dismissed them outright. Which, for an attorney, was a skill honed by years of practice and experience, both of which Robert had plenty of.

When they finally finished their excessive back-patting, for in Bree's mind that was all they were doing, Robert stood up, as if he'd had enough. Alan and the finalists all went to stand too, but Robert motioned them back down. "No, no, stay where you are. Have breakfast on the house. But I've got to run."

"Here?" Alan asked as if he was stunned. "You want them to have breakfast here in this room?"

"Yes," Robert replied as if he was somewhat irritated by Alan's question. "My treat." Then he looked at the finalists again. "It was a pleasure meeting all of you."

"It was a pleasure meeting you, too, Mr. Colgate," Deidra said as Robert began moving away from the head of the table. "You're the best there is, in my view," she added, and many of the others agreed, praising him verbally too.

Bree was stunned, however, when Robert stopped walking as he approached the side of her chair. When she looked up at him, and saw up close his big, compassionate eyes, smelled his fresh, clean scent, her breath caught.

"And how are you, Brianna?" he asked to the shock of everybody at the table.

"I'm good, sir, and you?"

"Doing better." Much better, he thought, seeing her again. "I was thinking about what we discussed yesterday. About those Mississippi boys."

Bree was mortified. "I didn't mean it the way it sounded."

"No, you were right. It is unfair. Patently so. But when you get down to it, what's the alternative?"

Bree thought about this. "Better lawyers for everybody?"

Robert frowned on this, as if he had given it considerable thought. "Oh, I don't think a lack of skill is the problem. A lack of morality, surely, of compassion perhaps? Giving it your all despite the limits of your reward?"

Bree nodded. "More attorneys committed to the cause of justice as its own reward, despite the financial circumstance of their clients. Yes, sir, that would do it."

"Yes," Robert said, placing his hands in his pant pockets, looking down at her chest and then back into her eyes. "I was thinking about that."

Bree could barely regulate her breathing when he looked back into her eyes. And the way they bore into her, with that almost lustful look he had displayed yesterday, made her seriously wonder if he meant he was thinking about her, rather than what they had discussed. She felt as uncertain as she felt exhilarated.

"Well," he finally said as if he was still unsure about something, "you take care of yourself."

"And you don't work too hard, sir."

Robert smiled, pleased with her concern. "I won't," he said and then walked away, around one table and then another, until he was out of the room.

Bree stared at him until he was clean out of sight, her heart thumping with a nervous, unsure delight. When she turned back toward the group, however, everybody, especially Deidra Dentry and

Prudence Cameron, was staring at her, and staring in a kind of frozen disbelief.

And just like that, just because Robert Colgate had singled her out, Bree went from being the least-feared among the mighty finalists, to the one to beat.

She saw him again two days later, and their get together, especially that night, would eventually change her life.

Her job that day was to shadow Bret Drysdale, one of the senior associates, as he attended court hearings, depositions, and settlement meetings. Instead of going to any hearings, or any meetings, he had her running errands all day, from one floor to the next, taking this document here and that document there as if any of these errand runs would help her in her quest to become a high-powered attorney for Colgate. She was bored to tears. Until, by early afternoon, she was asked by Drysdale's secretary to take a case file to the tower.

"To the what?" Bree asked, frowning, as she stood at the secretary's desk.

"The tower. The top floor. Mr. Colgate's office."

As soon as the secretary mentioned Robert Colgate's name, Bree accepted the file gladly and hurried for the elevator. She was still reeling from the way he singled her out in the executive dining hall. It was as if every one of her colleagues looked at her with respect after that. Robert

Colgate talking to *her*? To *Miss Mississippi* as they snidely called her. They couldn't fathom it.

In a lot of ways, Bree thought, as she stepped off of the elevator onto the top floor, neither could she. Not that she doubted her abilities, she knew in her heart of hearts that she was more than capable of holding her own at a place like Colgate. But it was just that she'd never thought the head of the company himself would bother to so much as give her the time of day. She wasn't an Ivy Leaguer. Her family didn't have money or position or power, they were, every one of them, dirt poor. And she certainly didn't see herself as some beauty queen who stood out in a crowd - even Alan DeFrame's horny behind made clear that she wasn't all that. But Robert still had spoken with her - at length, and had singled her out the next time they'd met. And, if Alan was to be believed, had selected her above more worthy finalists. It was as mystifying to Bree as if was to her colleagues.

"Hey, Bree, girl," Lois Peterson said with a smile. Until now, Bree had only known her as the busty red head she often saw in the cafeteria. She now realized that she was, in fact, the executive receptionist.

Bree walked up to her desk inside the suite of offices that encompassed one full half of the top floor, a suite that made up the many layers of what was loosely termed Robert Colgate's "office." Bree immediately saw, at the end of the wide corridor, that Robert's actual office door was open, and he was seated behind his desk.

"What brings you to the tower?" Lois asked her.

"A case file from Mr. Drysdale," Bree said, handing the file over, although her eyes were on the office at the end of the hall.

Lois shook her head. "Bret Drysdale is the most insecure senior associate in the entire firm. He always wants Mr. Colgate's personal paralegal to peruse his work before he submits it for final approval, as if that woman has time to check behind him."

"And he's supposedly this mighty attorney," Bree said, not at all caring one way or the other. "What can a paralegal tell him?"

"I'm sayin'," Lois agreed. She was a white woman with a deep-throated voice and a penchant for slang. Bree had nothing against her, although she'd heard she could be rude when she wanted to be.

Bree glanced toward the end of the hall once more. She wanted desperately to talk to Robert again, mainly to see if he would give her advice on how to succeed at a heavy-hitting firm like his. She knew it was risky - he could view her as too ambitious even for him, but her father had always encouraged her to take advantage of an opportunity as soon as it presents itself. And seeing Robert certainly presented her with an opportunity. "I see Mr. Colgate's in," she said to Lois.

"For a change, yeah. He's headed to LA this weekend. He's defending Jay-Pat on a murder charge. I never heard of this Jay person before, but my kids did and they're all excited."

Bree leaned closer, lowering her voice. "You think I can talk to him for a few minutes?"

Lois looked at her with suspicion and amazement. "Talk to Mr. Colgate?" she said far louder than Bree thought necessary. "You can't just talk to Mr. Colgate. Even I can't just walk up on him like that. He'll look at me like I'm crazy. What on earth do you need to talk to him about?"

"I had some questions, that's all."

"Well, girl, you'd better take those questions back where you got 'em from. Alan DeFrame will have your hide if he knew you were up here bothering Mr. Colgate."

Bree began to panic. Lois was taking it all wrong. "I'm not trying to *bother* him. I just had a question—"

"Alan will dress you down without mercy if he even thought you were trying to worm your way—"

"I'm not trying to worm my way anywhere. I was just . . . But you know what, Lois? Forget it. I'll talk to you later."

Bree moved away from Lois' desk quickly, angry that she was trying to floor-show on her that way and angry at herself for ever thinking that a loud-mouth female like Lois Peterson could be reasonable.

Bree stood at the elevator and punched the button repeatedly, anxious to get down from the tower as quickly as she could.

"Bree, hey," a male's voice could be heard behind her and Bree turned to the sound. It was Monty Ross, Robert's personal assistant and the man who had taken the finalists on a tour of the building. He was a small, handsome man with a low-cut Afro, oak-brown skin, and a wardrobe straight off of the pages of GQ. He walked up to Bree in his double-breasted, periwinkle blue suit.

"Hi, Monty," Bree said, attempting to smile and shield her embarrassment. "How you doing?"

"Good, good, it's all good. How's Alan treating you?"

Bree raised her eyebrows, refusing to lie.

Monty laughed. "Say no more," he said. "We all know Alan. The man is brilliant but man is he a pain."

Bree smiled genuinely at this. She wished at that moment that Robert would have put Monty in charge of his recruitment program. He, after all, used to be a law professor, a teacher of the law, and she knew she'd have a fighting chance if he was in charge.

"But listen," Monty said, his voice lowered, "Mr. Colgate would like to see you."

Bree was stunned by this. "Me?" she said, pointing at herself, and then disappointed with herself for behaving so hick-like. She should have simply said okay, as if it was no big deal to her.

"If you could spare a moment, yes," Monty said with all sincerity, as if Bree would consider turning down Robert Colgate.

"All right," she said in her best disinterested voice, and then followed him toward Robert's office. She glanced at Lois. Lois was staring at her.

Robert was on the phone when they entered his massive office. His eyes were closed as he pinched the bridge of his nose and listened to the person on the other end. Even though he didn't acknowledge their present, that still didn't stop Monty from depositing her inside the office, and then closing the door as he left.

Bree immediately felt uneasy. She wondered if Robert even realized she was there. But Monty, she decided, would not have asked her to come to see Robert if he had not ordered it. So she got a grip and looked around.

The office was huge, with floor to ceiling windows that overlooked the dreary Chicago skyline, and a sitting area alone that seemed larger than her entire hotel room. She looked at Robert. He seemed tense, as if the person on the other end of the telephone line was telling him something he didn't want to hear, and it was a shaky conversation. When he concluded the conversation by saying, *okay, Jake, see if you can keep a lid on it until I get there*, solidifying the fact that the person on the other end had given him either bad news or more work requiring his attention, Bree's suspicion was confirmed.

"Hello, Brianna," Robert said as he hung up the phone. Seeing her again seemed to ease his troubled mind.

"Hi."

"I'm not interrupting anything vital, I hope," he said. Then added, as he stood to his feet, "come and sit over here with me for a few minutes," motioning toward the sitting area. "I wasn't interrupting anything, was I?"

"No," Bree said, following him toward the sofa, "I was just running some errands."

"Working hard?" Robert asked, looking back at her.

"Yes, sir," she replied with a smile.

As they sat side-by-side on the sofa, Bree noticed that Robert was in shirt sleeves, and his arms were wide and muscle-tight beneath the white dress shirt. "Think you're getting the swing of things all right?" He crossed his legs, turned his body toward her. They were so close that their legs were within an inch of touching.

"It's coming along," she said, deciding to take advantage of what she feared could be her only opportunity. "I just don't think I know what Alan wants."

"He wants excellence," Robert replied, "or as close to it as anyone can come."

"We're shadowing senior associates now. All I've been doing all day is to take documents from one floor to the next."

"For?"

"Mr. Drysdale."

Robert nodded. "Has Bret impressed you yet?"

"Mr. Drysdale? No, sir," Bree said bluntly.

Robert laughed, pleased that she wasn't trying to flatter him. "Good," he said. "If you would have said yes you would have disappointed me."

"Why is he here?" Bree asked with all sincerity. "If you don't mind my asking. He seems so . . ."

"So incompetent?"

"Well, yes, sir."

"He is, of course. Has no practical sense whatsoever. Until you get him in a courtroom. He's a master in the courtroom. Jurors love him. He rarely loses a case."

This astonished Bree. "Why would jurors love him? I mean, he's nice and all, but I don't see what's so loveable about him."

Robert looked at her face, at her soft, dark skin, his voice growing faint. "He has what I think you have. And you can't teach that."

Bree's heart began to pound. "What is it?" she asked him, unsure if she really wanted the answer.

"Pity," Robert said.

Bree frowned. "Pity? They pity him?" Was he saying that jurors would pity *her*?

"Yes. They sympathize with him, understand him, see him as the little David against the mammoth Goliath. They will almost always side with the Davids of the world."

Bree didn't know if she wanted to go there, but she felt she must if she ever was to understand his interest in her. "And you see a David in me?"

"Yes," Robert said. "Royally."

"So you didn't see my skills or my abilities or even my potential. You just saw that I was pitiful and that did it for you?" Bree knew she sounded bitter, but she couldn't help it. She felt bitter. All of her life she was always pushed to the back, told that she wasn't good enough, never, as Alan DeFrame said, the winner.

Robert didn't respond to her bitterness. He simply continued to stare at her. He saw a lot more in her than he could perhaps even explain to himself, so it was for certain he wasn't going to try and explain it to her. Besides, his manhood was throbbing just by being this close to her, rendering his concentration a little off.

Although he was warring with himself inside, his outer calmness helped to calm Bree back down. "I thank you for the opportunity anyway," she felt a need to say.

Robert smiled. "Keep that fire, Brianna. It'll serve you well."

His eyes kept moving down to her luscious lips. And he wanted to kiss her. He wanted to do far more than that, but he had to kiss her. Just one kiss.

When she returned his gaze, and hers was as fiery as his, he knew he had to do it. He'd never done this before, he'd never in all the years of their training program allowed himself to so much as have one moment of private time with one of the trainees. But he'd never felt the way he felt when he saw Bree's video, either. He leaned forward. If she didn't resist him, he had to do it.

He did it. Because she didn't resist. Because their lips met and a fire shot through his entire body. It was a chaste, sweet kiss; he didn't want to scare her. But when their lips parted again, and he realized the feeling was even better than he had imagined, he had to kiss her once more. Just one more. And he did it. Another chaste kiss. Then another. By now he was so hot and had moved so close to her that he was almost on top of her curvaceous body. But with his final kiss, a kiss that was supposed to be as chaste as the others, his control broke.

His lips seared into hers, his tongue prodded and poked and intertwined into hers. He pulled her into his arms as he kissed her. And when she wrapped her arms around him, a guttural sound came from his throat and he bore into her. She was turned completely sideways by now, and his hand reached down beneath her skirt, into her panties, and squeezed her soft, tight ass. He rubbed and squeezed as he kissed her, as this young woman who did the craziest things to his heart allowed him to feel as if he had been accorded the honor of occupying a special place.

The buzz of his desk intercom caused the kissing to stop. Otherwise, he wasn't sure if he could have stopped. He was breathing so heavily when their lips parted, that he thought he was going to have a heart attack. And his hand still rested on her bare ass, as if it had melded onto her supple, pliable skin.

He looked at her. Although he saw some fear and alarm in her eyes, he saw happiness there, too. And when she smiled, his heart relaxed. "I'm usually not this aggressive," he said, and she smiled even greater.

"Somebody's trying to get in touch with you," Bree said. One of her hands had landed in his mop of brown hair while he had been kissing her, and was still there.

Robert rubbed her hair as well. "I guess I'd better see what they want." He slowly slid his hand from out of her panties, still massaging her butt as he did, and then he stood to his feet. "And you'd better get back to Bret, before he starts wondering what's become of you," Robert said.

Bree immediately blushed with embarrassment as she hurried to her feet. She hadn't meant to linger, or to give him the impression that she wanted him to check his intercom and then come back and fondle her. She wanted to tell him she didn't mean that, but knew it would sound ridiculous.

"Goodbye, sir," she said, about to leave.

But Robert grabbed her by the hand and held it. "Have dinner with me tonight," he said to her.

Bree looked at his hand, and then into his eyes. "Dinner, sir?"

Robert nodded. "Yes. At my place." He studied her. "I want to spend some time alone with you," he admitted.

To finish what I started here, Bree knew was what he really meant. "I don't think that's a good idea, sir," she said.

Robert smiled. "It's a lousy idea, are you kidding?" Then he turned serious, rubbed her narrow shoulder. "But it doesn't negate the fact that I want to spend some time alone with you."

Bree knew this was crazy, she knew she'd live to regret this decision, but she couldn't see herself turning him down. She liked Robert, liked him from the moment she met him. And she was no fool, she knew this could backfire on her and was more likely to hurt rather than help her career. Especially if it goes too far, and they end up in bed.

"Come on, Brianna," Robert said, "I promise you'll enjoy yourself."

Every ounce of her brain was telling her to turn down his offer, that she'd live to regret it if she didn't. But her heart told an entirely different tale. *You'd be a fool*, her heart was saying, to *turn this down*.

"Okay," she said, listening to her heart entirely.

Robert smiled, very pleased. "I'll send a car for you. They have you guys staying at the Omni, right?"

"That's right," she said as his desk intercom buzzed again. He kissed her lightly on her forehead, stared deep into what he could now see were troubled eyes. He knew this decision came with a price for her. "It'll be okay, Brianna," he said to reassure her. "You aren't doing anything wrong. Okay?"

Bree nodded, although that wasn't the reassurance she needed. She needed him to say, come to dinner, enjoy a fine meal with me, and I promise not to touch you. Of course she could always refuse his advances herself, although she knew what that could do for her career. But the way she felt when he was kissing her just now, the way he made her feel, kind of squashed any notions that she could ever refuse this man.

"Okay," she said, smiled weakly, allowed him to kiss her on the forehead again, and then she left his office. She was embarrassed and elated, confused and overjoyed, all at the same time.

Robert was concerned himself, after she left, as he walked toward his desk. How in the world was he going to manage this? He couldn't have

LOVING THE HEAD MAN

an affair with one of his trainees, that kind of
practice was something he'd never dreamed of
doing before. And to mess with somebody as
sweet and innocent as Bree. Was he corrupting
her? He'd be stunned if she was all that
experienced. She'd had a few encounters, a few
rolls in the hay with some of her hometown boys,
he could tell by the way she kissed him. But
nothing on the order of what he would want from
her. Which he knew he couldn't, shouldn't have.
Not with one of his young trainees!

His trump card, he also knew, was that he'd
be in LA this weekend preparing for the Patrick
trial, and would be tied up for quite a few weeks
to come. If he didn't see her, he couldn't fuck
her. So why was he seeing her tonight? Why had
he insisted on it to a point that almost sounded
like he was begging her? When he knew if he so
much as feasted his eyes on that young lady
again, on that particular young lady, there would
be no reprieves, no intercoms to interrupt, there
would be no turning back.

FOUR

"I'm in here, Brianna!" Robert yelled out as soon as Bree entered his penthouse apartment. He had buzzed her up and had told her that the door would be unlocked, so she had entered without knocking. Now she stood in a living room that was as large as she'd ever seen, filled with floor-to-ceiling curtain-less windows that overlooked the magnificent Chicago skyline, and she immediately felt different.

Chicago was a wonderful sight to see at night, Bree thought. In fact, as she followed the sound of Robert's voice through the living room, through the huge dining hall, and into the kitchen, the floor-to-ceiling windows were so prevalent that she felt as if Chicago's skyscrapers were as much a part of this home as the furniture, or even Robert himself.

Everything looked so rich and elegant to Bree, so outside of what she was accustomed to, that she began to feel a sense of accomplishment again. Which was odd since coming to Robert's apartment tonight, particularly with what she knew he had in mind for her, would hardly qualify as any kind of achievement. And especially not the kind she would go around bragging about.

The aroma of fresh, steaming vegetables met her as she rounded yet another corner and entered the classically-appointed kitchen. Robert was standing at the granite-top center island, chopping more vegetables and tossing them into a wok on the tabletop stove, when she entered.

When Robert looked up and saw her, looking so refreshing to him in her low-cut, spaghetti-strapless, pullover yellow silk blouse, her jeans and heels, he felt a sudden burst of warmth toward her. "Hello, there," he said with a grand smile. Although she looked pleased to see him, he could also still see a little apprehension deep within her big, expressive eyes.

"Hi, Mr. Colgate," Bree said, feeling a little more at ease when she saw Robert.

"Mr. Colgate?" Robert said. "No ma'am, not here. I'm Robert to you, young lady."

Bree smiled. "I stand corrected," she said as she began sitting on the center island stool directly across from him. "When you asked me to have dinner with you, somehow I didn't expect you to be cooking it."

"Ah, you expected a chef."

"Or takeout, yes."

Robert laughed. "Takeout, Brianna? Come on. Why in the world would you think I'd do that to you?"

Because nobody else had ever pampered her a day in her life. Because she was so not used to anyone going any extra miles for her. "It just never occurred to me, that's all," she ultimately said.

She looked at him as he worked. He wore a light blue, pullover V-neck shirt that gave wonderful definition to his stark blue eyes, and Bree feasted herself on his broad shoulders, his strong chest, his muscular arms. And not for the first time she wondered how it would feel to have a man like him easing his rob inside of her, making her wet, making her come. It had been so long since she last had had some, not since she was fooling around with Malcolm. Malcolm was an activist she'd met in law school who was recently hired at a Mississippi firm specializing in civil rights, who couldn't understand why she would want to leave their beloved state to try and get a job in the kind of elitist, corporate America he despised. And especially at a firm like Colgate's.

"They don't even do pro bono work, Bree," Malcolm had complained when she told him of her plans. "They only defend the rich and powerful, never the poor. And you want to work at a place like that?"

For Malcolm, becoming a lawyer was all about helping right the wrongs of injustices everywhere. For Bree, it was all about ending vicious cycles, about keeping her family from falling apart, about earning the kind of living that would ensure that her younger siblings didn't have to struggle too. It was all about keeping the promises she made to her father.

After Robert lifted the wok to give his vegetables one final toss, he lowered the heat to simmer, wiped his hands with the towel that was thrown over his shoulder, sat same towel on the countertop, and then gave Bree his undivided attention.

"You look pretty," he said, his eyes tracing her face and then moving down to her blouse. "I like that color on you."

Bree blushed to the roots of her hair when he said that. Was she being too obvious here, dressing in what was probably provocative clothing given her usual business attire? Did she like the attention he was giving to her, and was playing it up? That certainly wasn't her intention. She just wanted to look good tonight. For some reason, she didn't want to disappoint him tonight.

But she remembered what her father had said when she couldn't seem to accept compliments he would give to her. "Just say thank-you," he'd say, "and keep on truckin'."

"Thank-you," she said.

"How about a drink?"

"Sounds good."

Bree got off of the stool as he poured their drinks, and walked over to the opened French doors that led to the balcony. She leaned against the doorjamb and allowed the wind to blow through her braids.

Robert came up behind her. She felt his presence, could sniff his wonderful masculine scent, but she didn't turn around.

"Like the view?" he asked her, looking, not at the view, but down the length of her, imagining her body beneath his.

"Who wouldn't?" she said. "I could stand here all day, wouldn't get anything done. This kind of view would be very counterproductive for me."

Robert smiled. Handed her a drink. "Here's to you, kid," he said, lifting his wine glass.

Bree smiled, lifted hers, and they clanked.

And the evening was just as relaxing for her. Robert was the perfect gentleman, as he wined and dined her, told silly jokes and laughed at her sillier ones. It wasn't until later that night, after dinner, when they were seated on his living room sofa, when what she knew was the point of the evening all along began to take shape.

He had crossed his legs, with wine glass in hand, and was staring at her. She was up, checking out his CD collection.

"Jazz, jazz, and more jazz," she said. "Especially Thelonious Monk."

"He's a master," Robert said.

"Better than Charlie Parker?"

"Don't know if I'd go that far," Robert said and Bree laughed. And she sat down beside him.

"I like jazz okay. But I wouldn't go out and buy any jazz records or anything like that."

Robert turned his body toward her, and considered her. "What kind of music relaxes you?" he asked her.

"I don't have a favorite genre," she said. "Not really. I mean, I'm not much of a music person."

"Just work, work, and more work. Right?"

"Mostly, yeah."

"Too much work, Brianna--"

"I know."

"So if not music, what do you like to do to relax?"

The way he was looking at her, staring at her neck, her shoulders, her mouth, her hair, rubbing his cool wine glass against his forehead as he appraised her, made her well aware that his question was loaded for bear. "Several things," she said, staring back at him. The wine was giving her a buzz, making her too relaxed, too willing to sway to Robert's faint, but undeniable beat.

"Name one?" he asked her, moving closer toward her.

Bree smiled. She couldn't think of anything. "Several things," she said again.

"You know how I like to relax?" he asked her, moving closer still.

She looked at him. His eyes were by now lust-filled. "How?" she asked, her heart beginning to pound.

He sat his wine glass, and hers, onto the side table. "Like this," he said as he pressed his lips against hers, kissing her in small kisses, and then in a deep-throated, sensual slather. He loved the way she tasted, loved the way she made him feel so heady, like no wine in this world could give him this kind of buzz.

Bree loved it too, and relaxed in the enjoyment of him.

"And like this," he said, as he pulled down the spaghetti straps of her blouse, as her sizeable breasts popped out into what Robert saw as two beautiful black, juicy bulbs. He began kissing and licking them, squeezing them and sucking the nipples.

Bree leaned her head back, her neck fully exposed, as she felt the sensations rip through her entire body. He got down on his knees as he continued to kiss and suck her, and began to unbutton and unzip her jeans.

She didn't realize he had already unbuttoned and unzipped his own pants, his penis hanging out in a long, thick, massive erection, and had them bunched down below his knees, until she finally looked down. He lifted her small body when she looked down, and in one fell swoop slipped completely off her jeans, panties and heels, rendering her entirely naked from the waist down.

"And like this," he said as his head moved down and he began to lick and suck her stomach, her thighs, her mound, and ultimately, her womanhood.

When he began licking and sucking her womanhood, she leaned her body back on her elbows, unable to contain such sensual feelings, her body too ripe, too ready, too sex-starved to not grow wet with hunger. His tongue was expert, as he buried his head between her legs, as she grabbed his full head of silky brown hair in her hands to ease, to not ease, his explorations. She had never, not ever, felt this way before.

Robert knew he couldn't hold out much longer. Not the way Bree smelled and tasted and turned him on to such an extent that his manhood was expanding almost beyond his skin. He stood up and stepped out of his pants. He slipped off his shirt, revealing to Bree a body of iron abs and a penis so thick, so massive, that she almost licked her lips. She wanted this.

Robert wanted her too, wanted her even more as he kissed her womanhood, as he slid his fingers inside of her to moisture her, to feel the fit. She was tight and narrow, the way he loved it, but he was also concerned, given his massive size, that this may be too painful for her. He continued to prepare her.

Eventually he grabbed her into his arms, and carried this cherished woman into his bedroom. He knew he had to take it easy. His fear, his greatest concern, was that, given that it was Brianna, he wasn't going to be able to.

When he laid her on his bed and eased on top of her, he was able to take it slow and easy. He continued to kiss her, to suck on her, to pamper her with affection. And when he entered her, he entered so slowly that he began to drip before he was even halfway there. But by the time he was halfway in, and her wet, pliable body was allowing him passage further and further in, and he was catching his rhythm, his control broke. This was Brianna. This was the woman he had been thinking about, dreaming about ever since he saw her innocent face on that screen. And his movements quickened.

"Oh, Brianna!" he yelled in a guttural tone as he made love to her, as every muscle in his body fell prey to that sweetness between her legs.

Bree felt it too, as he pounded her. She had never dreamed being with him would be this intense, this emotional, or would feel this unbelievable. She screamed out too, as he pounded her, as she held onto the head board when he would not relent, as the intensity would not relent.

When the climax came, her body felt as if it was levitating. She arched her back in an almost catlike, acrobatic maneuver. He held her bare ass tightly against him, her legs wrapped in a death grip around him, as his penis made that final push so deep down within her that it seared her. And both bodies, eviscerated, exhausted, rammed back down.

The jet-black Mercedes stopped at the curb in front of the Omni Hotel. Robert, behind the wheel, looked over at Bree. He hadn't wanted her to leave, not after the kind of lovemaking that had stunned him in its intensity. And if an experienced man like him had been so captivated, he could only imagine how absolutely different Bree must have felt. She was so spooked, in fact, that she had decided to leave shortly thereafter. Robert was disappointed, he wanted to hold her all night if he could have, but he understood. Because he was spooked, too. And with his crazy schedule he knew he shouldn't dream of taking on this kind of intense, emotionally-loaded relationship at this time in his life.

"Thanks for the lift," Bree said, her hand on the leather door handle.

The idea of going back to his empty apartment, without Bree, made him suddenly feel lonely. And he couldn't help it. He wanted her. "The Patrick trial is set to begin next week so I've got to leave for LA this weekend. But I want to see you again when I get back, Brianna," he said.

Bree immediately began shaking her head. "I can't," she said with some distress.

"I know my timing is lousy. I know I'm engaging in behavior I never dreamed I'd allow myself to engage in. But Bree--"

"I can't, Robert," Bree interrupted him.

"But why not? I'm the boss. I give you permission."

"But I don't give myself permission," Bree said and looked at him. "I didn't come all this way to

Chicago for any heavy romantic affair; I'm just getting started in my career. I can't deal with this right now."

"You wouldn't have to deal with anything, Brianna, I'll take care of everything. I'll take care of you." He felt as if he was begging her.

Bree looked at him intensely. "Why?" she asked.

That one word threw him. "What do you mean why?"

"Why are you showing all of this interest in me? Pru, Deidra, many of them look better than I do. I'm no beauty queen. I'm smart, but so are everybody else here Colgate or they wouldn't be there. I have no background and breeding like the others do. So why me? Why would a man like you, who can literally have anybody he wants, want me?"

"Because I've had everybody I wanted," Robert said. "You're more than that to me. You're somebody I think I need."

If Robert thought his declaration was going to touch Bree, he was incredibly misinformed. It spooked her even more. She wasn't ready for this. She didn't sign on for *this*."

"You don't trust me, do you?" Robert asked her. "You think I'm some womanizer already with more women than he can handle, don't you?"

"No, I don't know, I mean . . . I just . . ." Bree looked forward, then at Robert again. "I have to make it on my own terms, not because you did me any favors."

Robert looked grim. "Is that how you see our relationship?" he asked her. "As some kind of twisted quid pro quo? You let me fuck you, and I'll move your career?"

"No! That's not how I see it at all." Then Bree frowned herself. "But that's how other people will see it."

"I don't give a good gotdamn what other people will see!"

"That's because you don't have to give a good gotdamn," Bree said. "You've arrived. You're a man at the top of your profession. I'm just getting started. Which is the whole point. We aren't anywhere near on the same level. When I get there, and if you're still interested, we can maybe look into it. But a relationship on these terms would have too much power on one side, and I don't know if I want to cede that much authority over my life to somebody else."

Robert stared at her. She was far wiser than her years, which, he remembered, she was only twenty-five. And he understood. "Okay," he said, nodding his head. Then he looked at her. Leaned over and kissed her lightly on her lips, remembering how fantastic she was in his bed, wanting her there again almost desperately. But he understood why she wouldn't want that. "Take care of yourself, Brianna," he said as he leaned away from her.

Although she had been preaching this gospel all along, the firm way Robert said his farewell still stunned her. It was as if the argument was over and he agreed with her. And now, just like that, there was nothing more to argue about. But what could she do? Agree to become his what? Booty call? Whore? Mrs. Right Now?

Bree stepped out of his Mercedes and headed for the hotel's entrance. She looked back as he drove away. Although she already felt regretful, she knew she was doing the right thing. No matter how she sliced it he was asking for something that would be great for him, and miserable for her. Because she saw it tonight, when he made such passionate love to her, when she felt his rod deep inside of her, that she would fall for this guy in such an emotional way, in such a complete, all-or-nothing way, that a mere sexual relationship would be nowhere near enough for her. Although such a relationship would probably be the only kind that would work for him.

FIVE

Over the next several weeks, Bree couldn't get that night with Robert out of her mind. She would awake at night wet and ready, desiring to feel him deep inside of her again. Or she'd see herself laughing and talking with him again, about jazz, about the law, about life. She had it bad. And to make it worst, she began to have problems at work because of her intimacy with Robert, problems that she knew she had bought on herself, but that was still taking on a life of their own.

Although Robert was still in LA defending that rapper in what was becoming a very messy trial, and she hadn't laid eyes on him since that night, word had already gotten around the office, at least among the administrative staff and the trainees, that she had spent the night with him. It wasn't completely true, she hadn't spent the entire night with him, but that was beside the point. Somebody had told them that she had been with Robert. Which meant Alan respected her even less than he already did, and the other contestants feared her more than they already should. Because previously they had only suspected that she had some inside track with Mr. Colgate. Now that she had slept with him, or so they were told, they knew she had the advantage. A very unfair advantage, they added.

And it wasn't just the finalists who saw that he supposedly favored her. Some of his own staff up in the tower was beginning to refer to her as *Colgate's girl*, which was nonsense and Bree knew it. She hadn't seen or heard from that man at all since that night, had, in fact, told him that an ongoing, intimate relationship was out of the question. But according to the gossip, Bree Hudson and Robert Colgate was an item.

The gossip became so pronounced that one morning, after the mid-terms were posted and Bree's score was the highest, with Prudence Cameron close behind, Alan called one of his quick meetings. They sat in the board room, all in small conversations, until Alan walked into the room. Bree was shocked, absolutely floored to learn that she was the subject of the meeting. Some people, Alan said, were questioning the test results.

"The results are accurate," he assured the finalists. "I graded each and every one of those exams personally. And as all of you know, Bree and I have never gotten along, and still don't. But those exams tested your critical thinking ability, your ability to logically assess some of the most difficult cases Colgate's attorneys were now encountering, and Bree's answers were the best. That's just a fact. However," Alan added, and Bree knew something unsavory was about to be spoken, something not good for her.

"I understand your concerns," he said, continuing. "I would be concerned too if I knew we had a female among us attempting to sleep her way to the top."

Many of the other finalists laughed, especially Deidra and Pru, who high-fived each other. Bree stared at Alan. "So I contacted Mr. Colgate, who's still in LA as many of you know, and explained the situation. He agreed that this kind of dysfunction could not persist in this program. He therefore turned over the entire selection process to me. I and I alone will make the final selection on who will achieve the fifty thousand dollar signing bonus and become a card-carrying member of Colgate and Associates."

Many of the finalists were applauding and cheering before Alan even finished, as if by their demonstration they were socking it to Bree even more. Bree's heart was in her shoe. If Robert had ceded all power to Alan, she was doomed. He'd let her come in second, her work was too excellent for him to do otherwise, but even if she were the best, he wouldn't allow her to win. He just wouldn't.

Her saving grace was that many of the other attorneys at Colgate, who weren't privy to any nasty gossip about her by the administrative staff and trainees, who didn't play around when it came to excellence, already knew of her legal mind and her excellent ability to problem solve. If they felt strongly enough about a trainee, they could make recommendations that had to be considered in the final analysis. She had to continue to work hard, and work even harder, to convince those attorneys that she was worthy of their recommendations.

After the meeting, when the other finalists had left to partner up with an attorney for the day, Alan asked Bree to hang back. Just to rub it in, she knew.

"So what do you think?" he asked her, as he stuffed papers into his briefcase, his stylish suspenders highlighting his slim form.

"What do you mean?" she asked him, standing before him, her small arms folded.

He smiled. "Thought you had a sugar daddy, did you?"

Bree stared at him.

"Yes, you did," he answered his own question. "You didn't think he'd do it, did you?"

Bree frowned. "Do what?"

"Pass the selection authority over to me. Give me the power to make the ultimate decision. You thought you'd sleep with him, and you'd have it in the bag."

Bree wondered if it was possible. Would Robert tell Alan about that night? "Did he tell you that?" she asked Alan, careful not to sound alarmed.

"Of course he didn't tell me that, you idiot! Why would Robert Colgate ever tell me anything about his personal life? I'm just one of his minions, just like you. Only you're so far down on that totem pole that the bottom's higher than you." Then he smiled. "But it's rich, isn't it? I mean, I've been trying to get you in my bed since you got here. You turn me down as if I'm diseased or something." He said this with bitterness in his voice. "Yet you jump into bed with Colgate--"

"You don't know if I jumped--"

"Yeah, you jumped all right! Cary doesn't lie."

Bree frowned again. "Who the hell is Cary?"

"The driver who picked you up, and drove you to Colgate's apartment. Cary doesn't lie."

"Because somebody picked me up and drove me somewhere doesn't mean I got in bed once I got there."

"Oh, you got in bed all right," Alan insisted. "If you were in Robert Colgate's apartment that night, you were in his bed, too. But the point is, now that I'm the final arbiter, you're screwed. You were betting on Colgate, when everybody knows he would make a lousy sugar daddy. Didn't you realize it too? I mean, he doesn't do the young thing, you see. You're too young for him. And none of his women look anything like you, not a thing, and every one of them would run circles around everything about you."

Then he laughed. "You lost your bet, Bree. You should have slept with me. Still can if you're so inclined," he added, looking down the length of her. "But you lost. You slept with the wrong man." Alan said this with a laugh. Said this as he grabbed his briefcase and left.

Bree just stood there. She didn't sleep with Robert to gain some advantage. She, in fact, always assumed it would be bad for her career if she slept with him. But Alan was certain that was exactly what she had done.

She shook her head. Wondered if he was right, if everybody was right, and she was just as bad as they claimed. Maybe she was in denial. Maybe she wanted to be employed at Colgate and Associates so badly that she was willing to do anything, just as Alan had said. Maybe she was deluding herself into believing she slept with Robert simply because she liked him, and wanted to, and her career had nothing to do with it.

She didn't know. She thought she did earlier, before everything went crazy, but now she didn't know. Then she dismissed all thoughts of it. Because what could she do about it now? She just had to work even harder, that was all. And had to pray unceasingly for some kind of remarkable, out of nowhere miracle.

The miracle, however, didn't begin to take shape until nearly two weeks later. Robert was back in town and was involved in yet another high profile murder case. This one involved Mark Brokaw, a wealthy Chicago doctor accused of poisoning his patients. Like all of Robert's trials, it was a media circus, too. It became such a celebrated case that Alan stopped work one day and escorted them all to the courthouse so that they could see Robert in action. Or, as Alan actually called it, "excellence in motion."

The courtroom was near-capacity. The only reason Alan and the finalists found seats at all was because of Monty Ross's insistence, declaring to the bailiff that they were a part of the defense team of lawyers and needed front row seats.

Bree, like everybody else in the gallery, couldn't take her eyes off of Robert. Although court was not even in session yet, she stared unceasingly at him. It had been over two months since that night and this was the first time she'd laid eyes on him again. He stood at the defense table with his reading glasses on, his immaculately tailored suit hanging on him as if it had been stitched on, reading over a document with the ease of a man in his own element. She had missed him. She missed their short but sweet conversations. She missed the way he enjoyed joking around with her about her southern background. She also missed those wonderful, private things he had done to her now sex-starved body.

When he walked over to where they all sat, to shake hands with Alan and talk briefly with him, she felt a pang of longing for him she had never experienced before. Although the other female finalists tried to play off their infatuation, glancing at him on the sly as he talked with Alan, Bree couldn't even attempt to front. She stared at him. At his polished Italian shoes. At his perfectly pleated pants. At the way his suit coat was open, hands on his hips, revealing that flat, ribbed stomach she remembered from that night. She had been attracted to Robert Colgate probably from the first moment she met him. But now it was unambiguous. She wanted him.

But, to her despair, he didn't seem to want her. For as soon as he completed his conversation with Alan, and they both laughed at some joke, he waved half-heartedly at the finalists as a group, looking more profoundly at the group of pretty Prada girls than at Bree, and headed back to the defense table. It was as if he was making it clear that his interest in her was over, that she had turned him down once, and there would be no second time.

Robert, however, was doing all he could to avoid displaying any interest in Bree. Not because he wasn't interested, but because he had heard about the rumor mill, about how some loud mouth driver had spread the word that Bree had been to his apartment. He had given Monty a serious cussing-out for hiring such a blabbermouth, and the driver was subsequently fired. But it still stung.

He knew Bree was hurting, and he'd give anything to stop her pain. Which meant, he knew, that he had to avoid even the appearance of any favoritism. Although, when he first saw her sitting in this courtroom, his entire body ached for her.

That night was an eye-opener. He still thought about it, still woke up with an erection remembering how wonderful it felt making love to her. He wanted her again, but he knew he couldn't go down that road with her. Because she was right. She would have to cede too much to him, and his crazy career, and that wouldn't be fair to her. But he still couldn't help how he felt.

Bree couldn't help her feelings, either, as she watched him work. Every time he would cross examine witnesses, it was as if she was watching a tennis match. Only her eyes didn't vacillate from player to player, but remained fixed on Robert. And once, when he was walking back toward the defense table and their eyes met, she could contain herself no longer. She smiled at him. But he didn't smile back, causing her heart to drop and her eyes to almost reflexively glance at Pru and Deidra, to see if they saw it, too. By the smirks on their faces, she knew that they had.

After court, when the judge adjourned for the day, Alan and the finalists were escorted by Monty into one of the attorney's rooms to await Robert. Alan thought it would be neat if they could critique Robert's day in court, but Bree knew that would be an exercise in futility. Who, she thought, was going to criticize Robert Colgate?

Robert walked into the small room looking depleted but rejuvenated too, as if he knew he had had a good day. And all of Bree's colleagues pounced, praising him unabashedly, with even Alan singing his praises.

Robert stood back and listened to all of the accolades, but his heart kept drifting to Bree. She'd never know it, he made it his business to avoid any eye contact with her, but she had his undivided attention. It took all he had not to get in touch with her when he returned to Chicago. And then the Brokaw trial started, and he was too busy. Because whenever he was involved in a murder case, he refused to be distracted by anyone. Even his sweet Brianna.

"And what about you, Miss Hudson?" Alan asked almost as a sneer, and everybody turned and looked toward the back of the pack, where Bree stood. "Do you agree that Mr. Colgate was perfection in motion in that courtroom, making no mistakes, as your colleagues suggest?"

Bree felt trapped as she looked at her envious colleagues and at Robert, whom she knew would respect her more if she was completely honest. Even though she doubted if he was going to like what she was about to say. But she said it anyway. "Not really, no," she said.

Alan and the finalists could not believe their ears. They stared at Bree as if they knew she had done it now. *Who does she think she is*, their exasperated looks seemed to say. Robert, however, stared at her too, only he was staring as if she had just proven why he singled her out in the first place.

"So you're denying my sainthood?" he asked jokingly, although no smile was on his face. "Are you telling me that my cross examination of the prosecution witnesses wasn't, in your estimation, perfection personified?"

All of the others couldn't help but smile at his choice of words.

Bree, however, remained serious. "Your cross-examinations were great," she said, attempting to ease her hammering heart, "they were withering. But I thought you were almost too tough on that one witness."

"Ah. Let me guess which one. The nurse's aide?"

Bree nodded. "Yes, sir. All she was there to do was to tell what she saw. She was walking on the floor, making her rounds, when she saw Dr. Brokaw come out of one of the victim's rooms. I mean, he was the victim's doctor, after all. And she just told what she saw."

"Yes," Robert agreed, now very serious. "But she also saw—"

"Him carrying a syringe," Bree said. "I know."

"The syringe that could have contained the poison that allegedly killed six people, including that patient whose room she had seen him exiting. That, wouldn't you agree, is very damaging testimony for my client?"

All of the other finalists agreed easily with Robert, with Alan leading the charge. Bree, however, frowned.

"Not necessarily," she said. "I mean, Mr. Brokaw is a doctor. He was, in fact, the victim's doctor. Why would it be unusual for him to be coming out of his patient's hospital room with a syringe?"

"Because, Miss Hudson," Deidra Dentry said as if she was talking to an ignorant child, "you're forgetting the common sense in all of this. Doctors usually let the nurses administer shots."

"And even if a doctor administers the shot himself," Prudence Cameron added, "he wouldn't leave the room with the syringe still in his hand, not the way she described he was holding it. That makes no sense. I agree with Mr. Colgate. That aide's testimony was extremely damaging to his client."

Bree could see Robert staring intensely at her, and she didn't know if he was inwardly hoping that she'd maintain her opposition, or inwardly seething because of what he may have considered, as the others did, was her fatal misread of what had actually transpired on that witness stand. She prayed that the latter wasn't true, but even if it was she stayed true to herself. "I still disagree," she said, "that a CNA seeing a doctor come out of his patient's room—"

"With a syringe in his hand," Pru added.

"— with a syringe in his hand," Bree agreed, "justifies ripping into her the way Mr. Colgate did."

Deidra, who viewed herself as the leader of them all, the automatic frontrunner despite her lagging test scores, slung her blonde hair back and shook her head. "You talk as if context means absolutely nothing," she said. "Dr. Brokaw wasn't coming out of just anybody's room. He was coming out of the room of a woman who was poisoned within the same time frame, that same day that he was coming out of that room. That's damning evidence in and of itself, and I'm amazed that you aren't sharp enough to see that fact."

Bree glanced at the others. They found her equally dull of senses. And Robert was staring so intensely at her. "I never said it wasn't damning," she explained. "What I'm saying is why beat up on a witness who has no axe to grind? It makes the defense look like a bully trying to cover up for the fact that she's a problem for his client."

"Are you certain," Robert interjected, "that she has no axe to grind?"

"Thank-you!" Deidra agreed.

Bree was thrown by his question, but not so thrown that she could not manage a comeback. She hated that she always ended up as the odd girl out. "Yes. I mean, I just assumed she was an innocent bystander."

"Wouldn't you agree," Robert said in a measured tone, as if he didn't want to offend her, but at the same time wanted to school her, "that a reasonable jury might assume the same thing if I were to treat her with kid gloves and take her testimony at face value?"

"Probably, yes," Bree reluctantly agreed. "But you treated her as if she might be the murderer."

"What's wrong with that?" Pru asked. "She might be."

Michael Nesmith, another finalist, shook his head. "Come on, Pru, that's nonsense."

"No, it's not," Pru said. "You don't know her and Bree doesn't either."

"It's ridiculous," Bree said. "If you treat every prosecution witness as if they had a hand in the murders, then you'll run the risk of looking like. . ."

"Of looking like what?" Deidra wanted to know.

"Of looking like you was a con, a gamer, somebody who was just trying to distract from the fact that your client may be a very bad man. You'll lose all credibility with the jury. Everybody can't have blood on their hands"

Robert stared at Bree. "No, they can't," he said. "Good point, Brianna. I'll keep that in mind going forward."

The intensity in the room turned onto itself as the others could not believe that Robert gave in to what they considered was Bree's nonsensical arguments. But before they could react, the door to the room opened and Monty peered inside.

"Excuse me ladies and gentlemen," he said in that precise tone of his, "but a moment, Mr. Colgate, please."

Robert looked at his assistant. "What is it?"

Monty stood erect and then entered the room, closing the door behind him. "It seems the prosecution, sir, is suddenly ready to deal."

"Wow," some of the finalists couldn't help saying, impressed.

Alan smiled. "I wonder why."

Bree, however, was alarmed. "But you aren't going to accept. Are you?"

Everybody looked at her with that, once again, *who does she think she is* look.

Robert looked at her. "No," he said. "I just like to play rope-a-dope with them."

"What's that?" Pru asked.

Robert smiled and excused himself, making undeniable eye contact with Bree as he left.

When he left, everybody looked at Monty. "As Mr. Colgate always says, when you have them on the ropes, play rope-a-dope. He's playing rope-a-dope. It's distracting and it gives them a false sense of insecurity when he turns down every deal they toss. They begin to wonder whoa, what's Colgate got up his sleeves this time? Then, they overplay their hands trying to one-up him, thinking that they may be losing, and eventually their entire case falls apart."

Bree grinned. "Brilliant," she said, as they all began to stand.

Once they were back in the board room, however, criticisms of Bree first came with some subtlety, and then fast and furious. Bree just sat there, listening. Even Alan joined in the fray, stating unequivocally that she should have never questioned Robert's techniques. He even went so far as to suggest that Robert was just being nice to her by saying she had made a good point. Who did she think she was, anyway?

Bree listened to all of them but didn't respond to any of them. She felt she knew Robert well enough to know that he liked honesty above all else. And no matter what Alan said, or how he felt that she was way out of line, she was going to remain true to who she was.

Less than three weeks later, however, she would find herself naked in a bedroom, waiting for Alan DeFrame to pound her, being anything but true to who she was.

SIX

It all started a week before the end of the program, the day after the finals, when that so-called favoritism Robert supposedly had toward her was put to the test. Although the grades would not be posted for another few days, the tension was on everybody's face. Bree, in fact, for the first time in her entire time at Colgate, had awaken late and therefore arrived late, walking into the twenty-first floor board room just as Alan was on yet another one of his rants about how unimpressed he was with the lot of them. As soon as he saw Bree tip in and sit down, he pounced.

"You may think you're the golden child around here," he said, "but I'll knock that luster off of you real quick if you show up late to my meeting again. Understood Hudson?"

Bree was mortified. What golden child? Was he listening to Lois Peterson and those staffers up at the tower? Certainly she nor Mr. Colgate had been going around claiming that she had any inside tracks to anything. Especially the way he'd been completely ignoring her. But yet there it was. Out in the open again. Alan DeFrame himself making it clear.

"Did you hear me?" he asked her, when she didn't respond.

"Yes, I heard you," she replied, stunned that he would have gone there. Yet, less than thirty minutes later, she herself had to go there in a move that she knew at the time would change what relationship she had with Robert forever.

It started when her cell phone began to vibrate against her pant pocket. When she pulled it out slightly to glance at the text message, and saw that it was her fifteen year old sister Candice urging her to phone home immediately, she stood and hurried out of the board room, despite Alan's glaring look.

Normally when she received a text message during Alan's lectures, she would let it slide. But normally it would be her mother, or her brother Ricky. Candice, although only fifteen, was easily her most reliable sibling. She would never phone unless it was serious.

Bree stood in the corridor outside of the board room and quickly phoned home. Candice answered on the first ring. Their mother, she frantically told Bree, had been arrested.

Bree's heart dropped through her shoe. "Arrested?" she said with loud astonishment and then, realizing where she was, lowered her voice. "When? *What for*?"

"It happened last night, but they didn't let her call none of us until this morning. She told us it was parking tickets they had arrested her for, and for us not to let you know, but when they still wouldn't release her, Ricky went down there."

"I thought Ricky was in jail."

"He was, but they dropped the charges."

Again? Bree thought. That brother of hers had more lives than a cat.

"She wasn't arrested for no parking tickets, Bree," Candice kept on. "She was arrested for selling drugs."

"Selling *drugs*?" Bree asked, astounded even more.

"For selling crack, that's what they told Ricky. And the bail bondsman said her bail has been set for one-hundred-thousand dollars, that's how serious this is. But he said we can get her out with ten thousand."

"Ten thousand?" Bree said. Where in the world were they going to get ten thousand dollars from? Then Bree shook her head. Selling drugs. She can't even imagine her mother doing something that nuts.

"I know she told us not to call you," Candice kept on, "but what else was we gonna do? She was probably selling them drugs for Ricky, to help him pay that child support so they wouldn't lock him up for being delinquent, I'll bet that's why she was doing it."

"That still doesn't make it right," Bree reminded her younger sister.

"I know," Candice said lowly, and Bree could just feel the pain in her voice. Their mother was the worse role model in America, and Bree hated that her younger siblings had to witness all of the crap her mother and brother had them witnessing. She exhaled.

"Is it certain she's guilty?" Bree asked her.

"Ricky says yeah."

Bree closed her eyes then opened them back up again. "I'll see what I can do," she said. "I'll try to get a couple days leave and come home. Take a look at the case."

This pleased Candice. She thought she had to bear this burden alone. But as soon as Bree hung up, she felt as if that burden was actually hers alone. Because the only person who could help her was the last person she should be asking.

She stood there, her phone against her chin, her heart growing faint by just the thought of what she had to do. But she knew she had to do it. She had no choice. It was risky, and could potentially end their friendship, if they still had one, but she couldn't just stand back and let her mother rot in jail. Francine Hudson was a lot of things. A lot of awful things. But she was still Bree's mother.

Instead of returning to the boardroom to ask Alan DeFrame's permission to take a few days off, or even a few minutes' break, she got on the elevator and headed for the tower, to Robert Colgate. She knew it could backfire in her face and he could not only tell her no, but declare her a gold-digging hustler who was no different than all the other users he often spoke about. But her back was against the wall. This was her mother in trouble, not just anybody. She stepped off of that elevator without giving it a second thought.

Robert was seated on the sofa in the sitting area of his office when Bree was allowed in. There used to be a time when staffers in the tower would look at Bree as if she'd grown fangs if she asked to see Robert Colgate. But now, because word had gotten around that Robert somehow favored Bree, even Lois Peterson buzzed Robert's secretary to see if she could see if Robert was available. Used to be a time when Bree's request would not have gotten past Lois, let alone Robert's secretary.

"Brianna, come in," he said jovially as she entered. He had on a pair of reading glasses, his legs crossed, a stack of papers on his lap as he was reading over each one. He looked up at her over his glasses as she approached him. He could see a difference in her as she approached. Gone was that affable, wide-eyed, curious Bree. A look of anguish was instead on her pretty face.

"What's the matter?" he asked her.

Bree felt awkward at first as she entered. The last time they'd been alone, he had taken her to bed in what was a powerfully intense joining. At least from her perspective. The only problem she had was that she didn't know his perspective. Given his sophisticated style and cosmopolitan reach, he probably didn't find their night together intense at all. Probably couldn't count how many females he'd bedded that way. She therefore decided to ignore the fact that she was, in the end, a Mississippi hick, and focus, instead, on why she had come in the first place.

"Hi," she said as she stood before him, trying her best to seem at ease.

"Hi yourself," he said. Then he patted the space beside him. "Sit down."

She frowned as she sat on the edge of the sofa beside him, the thought of her mother sitting in jail so disturbing to her that she could hardly contain her anxiousness. She crossed her leg and began shaking the leg she'd crossed, which she usually did when she was nervous.

Robert looked down at her shaking leg, remembering his rod between those legs, and then he looked into her face. "Are you going to tell me what's wrong?" he asked softly.

She looked at him, at the papers on his lap and the other piles of papers on the table in front of them. "I hate bothering you like this," she said. "I know you're busy."

"Don't worry about that. Just tell me what's happened."

Bree let out an anguished exhale.

"What is it?"

Bree screwed up her face. She wished to God there was another way, another person she could ask this favor of. But there was no other way, and certainly no other person. She looked at Robert and decided against beating around the bush. "I know this is crazy, and I could be kicked out of the program for this, but I need a favor. A really big favor." She said this and then looked intensely at him, to gauge his reaction.

A clouded look did come across his face, maybe even a look of disappointment, she thought, but he rallied quickly and maintained eye contact with her. "A favor?"

"Yes, sir."

"What kind of favor?"

Bree inhaled, tried her best to control her warring emotions. "Could you lend me some money?"

She asked it with bitterness in her voice, a tone she hadn't wanted to take, and again she stared at him to gauge his reaction.

If there was one, he was adept at hiding it. "You need money?" he asked her.

"Yes, sir."

He studied her. "A personal matter I take it?"

Bree nodded. "Yes, sir."

There was a pause in his manners, what seemed like a kind of momentary correction in his mind. But then he sat his glasses and the papers in his lap onto the table in front of them, and rose and began walking toward his desk. "How much?" he asked as he walked.

Bree exhaled. This was the crazy part. "Ten thousand dollars," she said with great pain in her voice, angry with her mother for forcing her into this kind of position and potentially ruining her future in the process. And she kept her eyes on Robert's reaction.

His walk slowed as soon as she announced the amount, and he glanced back at her, but he kept on walking. He went behind his desk, unlocked a drawer, and pulled out a large checkbook. There was another hesitation, as if he was wavering, Bree thought, but then he began writing the check.

Bree, feeling relieved and awful at the same time, stood and walked toward his desk. She could hardly believe he didn't interrogate her, didn't demand to know why.

"You aren't in court today?" she asked him, leaning against his desk, attempting to normalize an anything-but-normal situation. The idea that she'd ask for and receive ten thousand dollars from this man, from *any* man, without him forcing her to tell the full reason and thereby indict her own mother, astonished her. She couldn't take her eyes off of him.

He tore the check out of the book, walked around his desk, and handed it to her. She looked at the check, a check written on his personal bank account, not Colgate's, and looked back up at him. Love, gratitude, and anguish were mixed up together in her troubled eyes.

"Thank-you," she said, heartfelt.

"You're welcome."

"You don't know how much this means to me."

This pronouncement of hers seemed to make Robert uncomfortable. He crossed his arms and leaned against the edge of his desk. "No problem," he said.

"I'll pay you back every single dime."

"Sure," he said almost snappishly, as if she was overdoing it and it was beginning to annoy him. Bree had at first thought he was taking it very well. Now she knew better.

"I wouldn't have asked if I didn't really need it."

Robert nodded, as if conceding the point. "I know you wouldn't have," he said tenderly this time and Bree didn't know what to make of him. He seemed annoyed with her on the one hand, and powerfully concerned about her on the other. This was tough.

"Don't you want to know why I need it?" she decided to ask him. He was entitled to an explanation. She had fully expected to give one.

Robert thought about this. "I'm sure it's for a good reason or, as you said, you wouldn't have asked."

Bree smiled. He was still on her side, after all. "Thank-you, sir. Thank-you so much." As she turned to leave, however, she remembered her additional request. "Oh, and sir," she said, "I'm sorry to ask it, but do you think I could get a couple days off? I need to go home to take care of some business." She said this to help make clear that the money was indeed personal and necessary, but she also meant it. She really needed to get back to Mississippi. Ricky getting arrested was one thing. Ricky was always getting arrested. Her mother's arrest, however, could completely collapse their already fragile family.

Robert, however, wasn't as quick to intervene. "That's Alan's call," he replied. "You'll have to get with him on that."

It wasn't quite the answer she had wanted, but she knew not to push her luck. "Yes, sir. And thanks again. You don't know how much I appreciate this."

When he didn't respond, she began leaving again, her heart faint. Why good fortune could never come her way without strings, she wondered. She had a chance to make it to the top of her profession, to get a position with Colgate, and what happens? She had to ask the firm's head for money to bail her mother out of jail. If it wasn't for bad luck, she almost wanted to say, she'd have no luck at all. Until she heard his voice.

"Brianna?" he said, and she quickly turned back around.

"Sir?"

"If Alan denies your request, come and see me."

This warmed Bree's heart. She smiled. "Thank-you, sir," she said, and left.

SEVEN

The trip to Nodash, Mississippi was as painful as she expected it to be. And it wasn't just because of her mother's arrest. Thanks to Robert's much-appreciated generosity, she was able to get her out on bail. And although the evidence was overwhelming and her mother did indeed attempt to sell crack to an undercover cop, Malcolm, Bree's ex-boyfriend and the attorney she phoned as soon as she hit town, spoke with her public defender and he believes they might be able to get her off if she'd agree to snitch on her supplier. So all wasn't hopeless. Until they were all seated around in the living room of their small, family home, and Malcolm asked about the auction.

"What auction?" Bree asked, puzzled. She was seated beside Malcolm on the sofa, with her fourteen-year-old sister, Titianna, seated beside her. Candace was seated on the floor, and Ricky, her older brother, and her mother, were seated in the two flanking chairs. The rest of her siblings were outside playing. The house was already small, but with all of them in that tiny living room, it almost made Bree feel cloister phobic.

Malcolm looked at Bree. "You mean you don't know?" He was a handsome man, with a low-cut fade, walnut-brown skin, and glassy green eyes. He was the one who had called it off with

Bree, deciding that she was too ambitious, that any wife of his would have to put family first and forego any heavy duty career. Other than that, Bree thought as she stared into his beautiful eyes, he would have been perfect.

"What are you talking about, Mal?" she wanted to know.

"It's all your mother's been talking about since you phoned and asked me to talk with her PD," he said as he looked at Bree's mother. "I just assumed you already knew."

Bree looked at her mother. Francine Hudson was pushing fifty hard, and had a hardcore edge to her appearance, but she still had a nice figure and attractive face. She puffed on her cigarette, sipped from her can of beer, and shook her head.

"What's going on, Ma?" Bree asked her.

"I ain't wit it," her mother said. "You hear me? I ain't wit yo' shit today, Bree, I ain't wit it. Just spent all that time in some pissy-ass jail, you taking your precious time to get here, don't even think about looking at me like that!"

It always hurt Bree to her heart the way her mother would lash out at her, but it wasn't as if she wasn't used to it. "What auction, Ma?" she asked again.

"The house," Ricky said, which caused a stern rebuke from Francine.

"What you tellin' her for? She don't give shit about you and me neither!"

"She didn't have to bail you out," Candace reminded her mother, only to get rebuked also.

"You shut the fuck up!" Francine yelled. "You ain't nothing but a child. You don't know shit about shit so shut the hell up!"

Bree's leg touched her sister's arm. "What about the house?" Bree asked Ricky, certain that she would get nothing from her mother.

"She couldn't make the payments on the mortgage, so it's up for auction in a couple weeks."

"In nine days to be precise," Malcolm said. "That's why I asked if you had a game plan."

Bree thought he was talking about a game plan to secure her mother's release. That was why she said yes. But she was still confused. "But what mortgage," she asked. "Pop paid off this house before he died. And he left the house to me."

"The second mortgage," Ricky said. "Ma got Dad to sign the papers two years ago, just before he died."

"But he didn't know what he was signing. He was sick out of his mind."

Francine looked at Bree with a look that could bend steel. "You tryin' to accuse me of fraud?" she asked Bree.

"The house was supposed to go to me when Daddy died. He left the house to me. And you knew he was going to leave it to me. How could you . . ."

Bree was stunned. She couldn't believe her mother would be that irresponsible with the only thing, and she meant the only thing, they as a family had in this world. And it wasn't exactly the Taj Mahal. It was, in truth, a small, shack of a house but with a good roof, three bedrooms, and a big backyard. She looked at Candace. "Why didn't you tell me, Can?"

"I didn't know until last night, when I heard Malcolm talking to Ma about it."

Bree looked at Malcolm. "How much?"

"She has to have forty-four to keep the house."

"Hundred?" Bree asked, hopelessly hopeful.

"Thousand," Malcolm said as she knew he would. "She couldn't or didn't pay the mortgage, the bank therefore exercised its right to accelerate the Note, which, as you know, means that the entire loan, not just the back payments, became due. She's already received the Notice of Foreclosure sale, which gave her thirty days advance notice of the date of sale. There are only nine days left. And she has to have forty-four thousand dollars in nine days or bids will be open to the public and this house will most definitely be sold."

It felt as if a ton of bricks had fallen on Bree. She could hardly believe it. Her father worked his entire life to pay off this home, and just like that it was about to be taken away? "How could you do something like that?" Bree confronted her mother.

"Bree, don't," Candace said.

"You know what this place means to Pop," Bree kept on.

"Yeah, well, pop's dead, ain't he?" Francine said. "And I still had bills to pay. Ain't nobody round here taking care of me. TiTi, Candy, Ricky, all them sitting around here expecting me to hold down this household. You ain't helping."

"I just got out of law school, Ma, and when I got that expense check from Colgate I sent every dime I could to you, and you know that."

"Well that wasn't near 'bout enough, and you know *that*!"

But it was Titianna, Bree's younger sister, who brought it all back home. "What we gonna do, Bree?" she asked. "Where we gon' go if we lose daddy's house?"

Bree leaned her head back on the sofa. Life was so unfair, she thought, fighting back tears. Then she pulled out her cell phone, and called Alan DeFrame.

Two hours later, Alan DeFrame walked into Robert's office with news he didn't want to hear.

"One of the finalists is calling it quits," Alan said as he walked over to Robert's desk. "We just got the word."

Robert was seated behind his desk going over a document dump from the prosecution that required too much delicacy to delegate to his staff. The only person he did allow to assist him, Monty Ross, was at the conference table poring over documents as well. When Alan walked in and made his pronouncement they both looked up, with Robert staring at him over the top tip of his reading glasses. "This is rather late in the game, especially after the finals," Robert said. "Which one?"

Alan smiled, as if he could hardly contain his glee. "Bree Hudson," he said.

Robert frowned. "Brianna? She requested a couple days off. Why would she quit? You gave her permission to take a couple of days off, didn't you?"

"I didn't like it, and I told her she wasn't helping herself by doing it, but yeah, I gave her permission. The program folds in a few days anyway."

"Then why did she suddenly decide to quit?"

"I have no idea, sir. All I know is she called me from Mississippi and said she wasn't coming back. That's all I know."

Robert exhaled. "Okay. I'll take care of it."

"It's typical Bree, if you want my opinion," Alan added. "The program is already just about over, and here she is giving up the opportunity of a lifetime. I read her the riot act, sir. I was very upset."

"That doesn't sound like Bree to me," Monty said. "What reason did she give?"

Alan rolled his eyes. He never liked Monty and never pretended otherwise. "I just said she didn't give a reason. Didn't I just say that?" He looked over at Monty as if to make himself clear.

"All right, Alan," Robert said. "I'll take it from here. Thank-you."

It was a dismissal, and Alan knew it, but he left smiling anyway. The way Colgate was always pampering Bree and singling her out over and over again as if that country bumpkin was something special, irked him no end. As far as Alan was concerned, Colgate was getting exactly what he deserved.

Robert, however, had Monty pull up from the computer Bree's cell number from the finalists' demographics page and he was on the phone to Bree within minutes of Alan's departure. He leaned back in his executive swivel chair and pinched the bridge of his nose. He had so much on his plate that the last thing he had time for right now was drama. But he dialed her cell anyway.

"Bree's no quitter," Monty noted. "I don't care what Alan says."

Robert nodded his head. It was no secret to him that Monty liked Bree, almost as much as he did himself. And when she came on the line, and Robert heard that soft, almost melodic voice of hers, he closed his eyes. Why that slip of a girl pulled at his heartstrings so, confounded him still.

"This Bree," she said into the phone.

"This is Robert," he said to her.

"Oh. Mr. Colgate. Hi."

"What happened?" he asked her.

"Sir?"

"What's this I hear about you not coming back?"

Bree exhaled. "I've got a lot going on here, a lot I've got to handle, and I can't handle it and be there, too. But as soon as I get a job here, I'll start paying you back every dime I owe."

"What is it?"

"Sir?"

"Don't jerk me around, Brianna. What's going on down there in Mississippi that requires your full attention?"

There was a pause. "Just some family problems," she said.

"Such as?" He knew he was being intrusive, and he knew she was uncomfortable with his intrusiveness, but he wanted the full story this time.

"It's just something I've got to take care of."

"I'm not asking you again, Brianna."

There was a long pause. "My mother was arrested for selling drugs," she finally said.

Robert frowned. "Your mother?" he said, and Monty looked at him.

"Yes, sir."

"Well is it true? Was she selling drugs?"

"Drugs?" Monty asked, astounded.

There was another pause of hesitation by Bree. "Yes," she said. "It's true. I was able to get her out on bail, that's why I needed the ten thousand. But it's so much going on, I've got to stay here and hopefully get a job with the public defender's office--"

Robert frowned. "Public Defender? You said you wouldn't be caught dead as a criminal defense attorney."

"I know, but the PD's office is the only game in town around here. There's never any openings in the prosecutor's office."

Robert exhaled. She didn't realize it, but she had him under her little thumb, and he still couldn't explain why. He pulled out a pad and pen. "Had your mother been arrested for drug dealing in the past?"

"No, sir. Never! She's never even been in jail before."

"What's her name?"

"Whose name?"

"Your mother."

"My mother, sir?"

"Yes, Brianna. What is your mother's name?"

"Francine Hudson."

"And her PD?"

"Sir, I know you're very busy and have a lot going on right now--"

"What is her PD's name?" His tone was firm, definitive.

"Jerry Kurtz. But really, sir, I'll take care of it."

"The only thing you're going to take care of is finding which flight you can get your ass on and get back to Chicago. Got it?" Then he exhaled. He really hated speaking to her like that, but her staying in Mississippi was not an option. "I'll take care of your mother's situation," he added.

"I can't ask you to do that!"

"You aren't asking me. I'm taking care of it. Just get back here." He knew he sounded almost desperate to see her again, which wasn't quite true, but he nevertheless didn't bother to look at Monty.

"Sir," Bree said, "I appreciate everything you're trying to do, but I don't see how I can just leave here now."

"Brianna?"

Yet another pause. "Yes?"

"Would you agree that when it comes to criminal cases I know what I'm doing?"

"Yes. Of course you do!"

"Then trust me to take care of your mother's situation, and get back here. All right?"

It took another pause, but she eventually relented.

When Robert hung up the phone, he looked at Monty, certain he would be staring at him. When Monty wouldn't say anything, but continued to stare, Robert gestured with his hands in a shrugging motion.

"What?" he asked.

"She's young, Bobby," Monty said.

Robert stared at him. Was it that obvious that he had a soft spot in his heart for Bree? He hadn't given any indication in that direction, at least Robert didn't think he had. "I know that," he said.

"She's not worldly and sophisticated."

"I know that, too."

"She won't dismiss your gesture. She'll take it to heart."

"So what do you suggest I do? Let her stay in Mississippi? Forget about helping her mother? I thought you were fond of Brianna."

"I am fond of her. And of course you should help. But—"

Robert frowned. "But what, man? Spit it out."

Monty hesitated before responding. "You have a reputation," he finally said.

Robert smiled. "A reputation? Oh, really now? And what exactly is this reputation of mine?"

"Of not being careful with young girls' hearts."

Robert frowned. What was he talking about? He didn't even fool with young girls. If he bothered to go down that road with Bree, and that would be a big if, she would damn near be the first. And she wasn't exactly a kid herself.

"I don't bother with young girls," he said.

"You know what I mean. Young women. Just don't lead her on, that's all I have to say. You have that black book of yours too full already.

Don't add Bree to your list. A sweet kid like her deserves better than that."

Robert looked away from his assistant, the truth of what he said embarrassing him. Then he pulled out his chirping smart phone.

"Mind your own business," he said. And then added: "Get the DA who handles Nomad, Mississippi on the phone."

"Nodash," Monty corrected.

"Whatever," Robert replied, and answered his cell phone call.

Monty smiled, he knew Robert well enough to know that he'd do right by Bree in the end.

EIGHT

She arrived back in Chicago the next day. She kept expecting Robert to send for her, or at least phone her all that day, but the call never came. It was as if he demanded her return, leading her to think that there was some serious interest again, but then as soon as she returned, he forgot about her. He did help her mother, however, miraculously getting the charges dropped for what the DA said was a lack of evidence, which even Bree knew was nonsense. There was plenty of evidence. But Robert had personally intervened and the DA dropped the charges. And for that alone, Bree would be forever grateful to him.

But by the second day of her return, the day before the final exam scores were to be posted, she knew she had to do something. In a matter of a week her father's home would be confiscated and her family would be out on the streets. She had tried to secure some kind of loan while she was in Mississippi, based on the kind of earnings her law degree could eventually net for her, but no bank, no loan company, no nothing, would bite. Especially not in the short turn around she would need.

As she entered the revolving doors of Colgate's downtown office building, she thought about going directly to Robert, to tell him the true state of affairs regarding her family home and ask him to lend, not give, but lend her the forty-four thousand they needed. But she nixed that idea as soon as entered the lobby and saw the mass of flesh coming and going and yapping on cell phones. This was the big leagues she was playing in now. And going to the boss over and over for money, wasn't going to cut it.

He might understand it. He knew how poor her family was and how tough times had to be for them. Or he might decide she was just another gold digging sister seeking to use him to enrich herself. Which would repulse him, she knew it would. She couldn't take that chance.

And she didn't have to take the chance by the time she arrived on the twenty-first floor and found the place abuzz with news that she and the other finalists weren't yet privy to, but that all of them, as they sat around in the board room and waited for Alan to come and give them instruction, knew was big. So big that Alan's secretary came into the board room, notified them that Alan was called to the tower (code speak for Robert's office on the top floor) and would be delayed for some time, perhaps all day.

Prudence, still reeling from having the second highest score total so far (although she was only three points behind Bree), looked at her cohorts and snorted. "All day?" she said in that condescending tone Bree had grown to hate. "What's up with that?"

But nobody was telling them a thing. All they were told to do was to stay busy, helping any associate attorney who needed help. Of course they all always did. Bree, however, needed to get to Robert, to see if she could at least feel him out about possibly helping her. She therefore hurried to Bret Drysdale's office. He was one of those associates who always had documents Robert's office needed to scrutinize. And within moments of Bree walking into his secretary's office and asking if they needed any assistance, she was handed a stack of reports they needed to get to the tower ASAP. Bree smiled, her instincts were dead on, and hurried for the top floor.

The elevator door binged open to a mad house. Robert's office, which comprised half of the entire floor, had so many of the firm's top attorneys coming and going, answering phones and quizzing each other, that Bree stepped off of the elevator feeling as if she had just stepped into a parallel universe. *What in the world,* she wondered.

As she walked toward Lois Peterson's desk, she could see Robert in the middle of the madness, standing behind his desk, his face strained and exhausted already and it was only ten am. She sat the documents from Bret Drysdale's office on Lois's desk, all the while not taking her eyes off of Robert, who was too busy listening to his slew of advisers to even notice that she stood at the end of the hall.

"Hey girl," Lois said to Bree.

"What in the world is going on?" Bree asked.

"You haven't heard? About the Vice President, I mean?"

Bree looked at Lois. "The Vice President? I didn't know Colgate had a VP."

"Not Colgate, silly," Lois said with a grin. "Jason Bradford. The former Vice President of the United States."

Bree was stunned. "Jason Bradford? What about him? What's happened to him?"

"Our gorgeous ex-VP has been arrested for raping some woman, and I mean violently raping her. The story broke on MSNBC last night. I was glued to the TV, girl, and you knew nothing about it."

After Bree got home last night, she was glued to her bed. "But what does Jason Bradford being arrested have to do with Colgate?"

Lois smiled. "Guess who his lead attorney is?"

Bree stared at Lois as if she had just grown fangs. "You're lying! Mr. Colgate?"

"Yes ma'am. Our Mr. Colgate is the lead attorney for the former vice president of the United States of America."

Bree once again watched Robert's hyper-busy office. "Wow," was all she could say.

"Ain't it surreal, girl?" Lois asked, watching the swirl of activity too. "He's the most envied attorney in the country right now."

Bree looked once again at Robert, concerned by the drain she saw all over him. "But what about Dr. Brokaw's case?"

"He's already reassigned that case to Milt Landon. Defending Vice President Bradford is going to be the only case he can even think about working right now. I mean, think about it, Bree. The former vice president of America can go to prison if he's convicted. It's crazy!"

"It's huge," Bree said, staring at Robert. She knew there was no way she could even bring up her problems at this point. "Doesn't Jason Bradford still live in DC?"

"He lives in West Virginia, but he has offices in DC. And he was arrested in DC."

"I guess Mr. Colgate will be heading there soon," Bree noted.

"They're readying the company plane as we speak," Lois informed her.

Bree kept staring at Robert, as if willing him to look at her. And finally he did, their eyes locking in a tense quick second. But as soon as there appeared to be a connection, Robert's private phone line rang and he snatched it up. "Colgate here," he said into the phone as the noise in his office began to ebb somewhat. Then he added, seeming to stand erect, it seemed to Bree: "Good morning, Mr. Vice President."

Suddenly his entire office went pin drop quiet and one of his top attorneys immediately hurried to the door and slammed it shut, effectively leaving Bree and Lois and all of the other staffers, completely out of the loop.

"Oh, well," Lois said, taking the documents Bree had given her and putting them in a manila folder, "prepare for the media frenzy."

Bree tried to smile, to feel the excitement that now encompassed all of Colgate as if it were a sort of bonfire of the vanities they were dealing with, but all she could think about was Robert. Once again it was too complicated, too *huge*, for him to say no. Once again, he was wearing himself too thin. Once again, Bree also thought, she was on her own.

It couldn't have been clearer later that same afternoon, when Bree had finally returned to the board room to collect her things and go home. Alan, standing in the doorway of his adjacent office, asked to see her. He did this periodically, to annoy her, in her opinion, but this time even she could tell the difference when she entered his office and closed the door as he had instructed. He wasn't harsh as he usually was. He was gleeful.

"I'm sure you've heard the news," he said, leaning back in the chair behind his desk and twirling around a stress ball, "about our naughty VP?" He looked at Bree grinning, as if he had just said something clever.

Bree's expression remained unchanged. The best way to handle Alan, she knew by now, was to never give in to him, never feed that beast.

"Which means," he went on, "that our Mr. Colgate will be otherwise engaged for a long, long time to come."

"It's late, Alan," Bree said. "Could you please get to the point?"

A harsh, angry expression crossed his face, although he attempted to smile it off. "The point," he said with an acid lace to his tone, "is that our program is winding down. In four more days the winner will be announced and this will all be over. And it's crunch time, Bree. There's not even going to be any recommendations allowed. Did you know that?"

Bree wasn't stunned to hear it, but she refused to show it. "No, I didn't," she said calmly.

"Well, now you know. I am not allowing any recommendations. Which means, of course, that you and Pru are the leading two contenders."

Bree stared at Alan. "Your point?"

"You, Pru, and Deidra are neck n' neck. It could go either way. In a matter of days, one of you will have a fifty thousand dollar signing bonus deposited in her bank account, and a position here with the elites, while the other two will get to go back home with absolutely nothing. That's a big deal, Bree. Can you imagine what you can do with fifty grand right off the bat? And then, to top it off, you'll start adding a six-figure salary to the pile, not to mention the prestige and advantages of working at Colgate that will automatically bring you. I mean, this is dreamland we're talking about."

He wasn't lying there, Bree thought. It would be the dream of dreams for her. Not to mention how easily it would solve the problem of keeping her father's house from the auction block. But Alan was up to no good, she could see it in his murky blue eyes. "So what are you saying?" she asked him. "That it's all between me and Pru?"

"You, Pru, and Deidra, yes."

"Deidra?" Bree asked with a frown. "But Deidra's test scores haven't been great, and her legal mind always accepts the obvious and isn't supple enough to go beyond the surface."

"That's your opinion," Alan said, although he and Bree both knew why gorgeous Deidra was making the final three cut. "But that's not my opinion. And my opinion is the one that matters. You know why? Because, contrary to what you may think, Mr. Colgate has put me solely in charge of the selection process. It's one hundred percent my decision."

Alan had already told the finalists about that, so that wasn't exactly news to her.

"However," he went on, staring at her breasts, "I will decide in your favor, Bree, and decide without hesitation, if you give me what I want."

Bree attempted to play dumb. "And what exactly is that?"

"Ah come on, Brianna! The airhead act doesn't do you justice and I'm way too smart to fall for it." His look changed. "You know what I want. You know I've wanted it since the moment I laid eyes on you. I want to fuck you, that's what I want."

This was Bree's opportunity to see if her suspicions were right. "Aren't Pru and Deidra and those other pretty Prada girls giving you that already?"

"Pru, are you kidding? Who the hell wants that prudish bitch?"

"Deidra then, surely."

Alan smiled. "Oh, yes, Deidra is available to me anytime I want her. Only that kind of easy lay takes the excitement out of it, know what I'm saying? So forget about her," he said. "If you give me what I want, you're in. No ands, ifs or buts about it. You're in."

"I want in," Bree admitted, "but never like that."

Alan frowned. "How else do you think you're making it in? Everybody has to give a little, what's your problem? You think you're too good to give it up to somebody like me? I'm giving you the ticket. Free and clear. One night with me, and you'll in. Guaranteed."

"No thanks."

"No thanks? Are you kidding me? You should be honored."

"Bye, Alan," Bree said, turning to leave.

"You think he's going to look out for you, don't you?"

Bree hesitated, and then turned around. "Pardon?"

"You think Robert Colgate is going to take care of you."

"I don't think any such thing."

"He's gone, sweetheart. To our nation's capital. And he ain't coming back any time soon, dearie, so any ideas you may have had are out the window. Besides," Alan added with another grin, "he's taking care of too many now as it is. You may as well get in line."

Bree rolled her eyes and walked out, determined not to show her devastation.

But life got in the way, and it was far more devastating than Alan's proposal. She spoke later that day to her mother, who begged Bree, like Candice, like Titianna, like Ricky, to do something. They were in panic mode now. She couldn't let them lose the house and become homeless. She just couldn't. It was up to her, they begged. It was on her shoulders and she had to do something!

And she did, the very next day. She tried every way she knew how to get in touch with Robert, or even Monty Ross, who was with him in DC. But those who would didn't have it, and those who could, wouldn't dream of giving Bree the time of day, let alone their boss's cell number. Then she begged them to contact Monty, and ask him to call her. But they wouldn't even do that. Not the associates. Not the administrative staff. Not even Lois. He wasn't even taking business calls from this end, not right now, as he was in serious negotiations with the DA to keep the vice president out of jail, and his days were long and too complication for them to dream of bothering him. She asked everybody she could, but nobody would help her.

And as the days grew closer to auction day, and even closer to selection day at Colgate, she knew she could not allow her father's home, a home he worked over thirty years to pay off, to be sold so easily, and her mother and siblings become homeless.

Although it was the most painful conclusion Bree had ever made in her life, she knew she had run out of options. Her back was literally against the wall. And for that pitiful reason alone, she walked into Alan's office the day before selection day, and accepted his sick, perverted proposal.

"How can I be sure," she asked him, "that you won't sleep with me and then stab me in the back by picking Pru or Deidra or somebody else?"

Alan smiled that reptilian smile of his Bree despised. "That's always a possibility of course," he said. "All I can tell you is that you have my word. You make love to me tonight, and tomorrow I announce you as the victor. As simple as that. The kind of transaction that happens all the time at our level of the game. You have got to trust me on this, Bree. You have got to trust me enough to know that I'll keep my word. Which, by the way, I will."

Bree wouldn't trust him as far as she could push him, but there were no better ideas around. And she hadn't heard a word from Robert. Not one word. That was why, later that same night, she found herself from there to this, standing naked in the living room of the company condo, as Robert walked through that door.

"*Brianna*?" he said, stunned beyond belief.

NINE

Robert and Bree both seemed so traumatized by what they were witnessing that moments passed before another word was spoken. And even then it wasn't either one of them, but Alan, who broke the silence when he came up front, stark naked too, calling Bree's name.

"Mr. *Colgate*?" he asked, backing up and covering his manhood with his hands as soon as he saw Robert, his voice nearly breathless with shock, as if seeing his boss before him had knocked the wind out of him. "What are you doing here, sir?" He tried to smile, he tried to lay on that DeFrame charm thick, but it was a hard sell in his position.

Robert, in fact, didn't even respond to Alan. He was too busy staring at Bree. Bree was so anguished, so crestfallen that she wanted to die where she stood.

"I was going to phone you," Alan continued, as if he could fast-talk his way out of this. "Just wanted to make sure you were okay. It's been like a feeding frenzy with the media, it's been ridiculous. The former Vice President of the United States accused of rape is a big deal, I know it's a big deal, but give me a break. Wall to wall coverage, twenty-four seven? I know you have your hands full. I was going to phone just to check on you. And just like that here you are."

He grinned. "Given the pressure, I thought you'd still be in DC."

Alan's casualness, his almost calculated coolness, disgusted Bree even more than she already was. He was behaving as if nothing at all was wrong, when anybody with eyes could see that everything was wrong. Including Robert, whose coolness, unlike Alan's flippancy, was chilling. He walked in further and closed the door behind him. And Alan, to Bree's shock, started right back up again.

"It's like an out-of-control monster of a case, isn't it, sir?" he said to his boss, determined to use his infamous sleight-of-hands abilities to change the subject. "The media's been brutal. Bret Drysdale is even publicly questioning if Colgate should have taken it on given the crazy publicity. But me and a few others went to Bret and told him he was out of line, I'm sure Monty briefed you on it. I mean, the vice president's been convicted already in the court of public opinion. Not his lawyer's law partners too." When it was obvious Robert wasn't entertaining anything he was saying, Alan went back to his moot point. "I thought you were still in DC, sir," he said.

While Alan continued with what was sounding more and more like nothing more than nervous chatter, Robert continued to study Bree. Bree felt like a carnival act, where Robert, like any other gawker, was waiting for the gimmick to show itself. His eyes were clouded by anger, Bree could see that, but his disgust was even more searing.

And without saying a word, he walked up to her, with Alan backing up slightly behind her. He removed his suit coat, and placed it around her naked body. His face was grim and drained as he pulled the coat lapels together, effectively covering her nakedness. She didn't realize that she had dropped every piece of her clothing from her hands, when he first walked through that door.

"What's going on here, Brianna?" he finally asked her.

It wasn't just that he looked exhausted - he was lead counsel in what many courtroom observers were calling the case of the century - of course he was going to look exhausted. But he looked sad, too, Bree thought, almost depressed, as if the one event he had dreaded ever coming true was upon him. Bree felt even worst just seeing that look on Robert's face.

Alan, however, remained clueless. "Nothing's going on," he quickly answered as if Robert had asked him the question, his nervousness now bordering on desperation. He was in trouble, and he knew it. "It's nothing like what you think, sir. We were just going over some interrogatories Bree needed help with. She was trying to understand—"

"You heard me, Brianna," Robert said, still ignoring the younger man. "What's going on?"

Bree wanted to deny it all. She wanted to give some long-winded explanation about why she had consented to do what he obviously thought she had done, but she couldn't pull herself to go there. Robert Colgate was no fool. She could tell any hard luck story she wanted, but at the end of the day the ending would be the same: she'd planned to sleep with Alan DeFrame. "I was supposed to sleep with Alan in exchange for being hired at Colgate and winning the bonus," she said to him, her eyes meeting his.

"No," Alan protested. "She's just playing, sir, she knows that's not the truth!"

Robert's jaw tightened. Although his eyes still held that coolness, the hurt, the pain was more evident now. It was such a searing pain that it made her want to yell from the top of her lungs that she wasn't that kind of girl, that it wasn't as base as it looked. She didn't plan to do something like this for the hell of it or just to get a great job. She'd never do it for those kinds of reasons. But who would believe her? It would be like a hooker yelling she wasn't a prostitute.

"We were going over some interrogatories," Alan kept on in some last ditch effort to win the day. "We had been working on this test case for the last few weeks and she thought she'd come up with this prototypical response to the Burlington decision—"

"I was supposed to have sex with him," Bree said bluntly, harshly, interrupting Alan's silly lies.

"I had agreed to come to the company condo, where Alan was able to borrow the key, and have sex with him."

Alan responded with such amazement that Bree could barely believe it. "Why you keep saying that?" he said as if it was Bree who was telling silly lies. "Have sex?" he said. "What are you talking about, girl? Sex? *Sex*? Are you out of your mind?" He actually grinned. "She's just joking, Mr. Colgate. I wouldn't–"

"Alan?" Robert said, his eyes still refusing to leave Bree's.

Alan swallowed hard. He knew that tone. "Sir?"

Robert looked at him. "Does it look like you're convincing me?"

Alan's heart dropped. He ran his hand across his blonde hair, finally ready to admit the obvious. "Okay, sir, it's true, we did come here for that, but nothing happened, sir. I wouldn't let it. And it had nothing to do with any selection. Bree was attracted to me, and I was attracted to her, so we decided to hook up. That's all this is about, sir, and she knows it. But I changed my mind, sir. Nothing happened." When he could see he was still getting nowhere fast, he exhaled. "I promise you, sir, coming here like this, it won't ever happen again."

Robert looked at him as if he had just birth a baby. "Won't happen again? That's the damn truth. I know it won't happen again. Because you're fired."

Both Bree and Alan were floored. Especially Alan, who looked as if he had just endured a body blow. "Fired?"

"Effective immediately. Get your clothes and get off of this property now."

"But, sir—" Alan pleaded.

"Get your shit," Robert said, his anger on the verge of breaking loose, "and get off of this property now."

Alan was devastated; Bree could see it all over his face. But it wasn't like he didn't get exactly what he deserved. The idea that he would give her the prize only if she agreed to sleep with his slimy behind was morally reprehensible. For him as well as her.

As soon as he began heading for the bedroom to retrieve the rest of his clothing, his body language unable to conceal his defeat, Bree turned to leave too. She needed to get out. To think. To get away from her own devastation. As soon as she moved to retrieve her clothes, however, Robert gripped her by the arm and moved her back in front of him, and he didn't do it lovingly either.

"Where do you think you're going?" he asked her.

"I need some fresh air."

"Did I tell you you could leave?"

Bree hesitated. There was an undercurrent of nastiness in his anger now. "No, sir."

"You'll do what you're told," he said, his hand still grasping her arm.

Bree's heart began to pound. She knew what he was doing. He wanted to rub it in. It was bad enough that he had seen her at her lowest; that he had caught her in what he had undoubtedly convinced himself was some kind of grand scheme she had been cooking up from the moment they met. He wanted to exonerate himself for having any interest in her to begin with, as if he knew all along she was a snake but was waiting to see just how she'd sizzle.

Alan returned to the living room fully clothe. And just as Bree suspected, his old arrogance had returned. He was already fired. He had nothing left to lose. "I'm not blowing my own horn, sir," he said, his smile now non-existent, "but I've had excellent results for Colgate ever since I've been there. And I've had better trial results than some of your senior partners, sir. Not to blow my own horn."

"Then stop blowing it," Robert said. And then he exhaled. "You'll get a letter of reference," he said, rubbing his forehead, "and it will outline all of your accomplishments while you worked for me. But you can't have any more association with Colgate."

"If it was any other finalist," Alan boldly asked his former boss, "would I even have been reprimanded?"

Robert stared at Alan. "What kind of question is that?"

"Because it's the truth. Because it's your fault."

"*My fault*? Your sleeping with Brianna is my fault?"

"He didn't sleep with me," Bree made clear.

"You elevated her profile, sir," Alan said, ignoring her. "And it made me curious. Hell, yeah, it made me curious. I mean, why were you so interested in her? She was cute and had some nice curves, but so did a ton of other females at Colgate and you never showed any interest in any of them. But you were so interested in Bree. You always wanted me to report back to you about Bree. 'How's Brianna?' you was always asking me. 'Make sure you stay on her. Make sure you let me know if her work product starts falling off.' And I would see the way you would look at her every time I was talking with you and we saw her walking by. So I figured what was it about this girl that would have Robert Colgate's attention like this? Damn straight I had to tap it."

Bree was floored by what she had heard, the idea that Robert was *that* interested in her, but she was not so thrown that she couldn't see how Robert's jaw tightened at Alan's admission of "tapping" her.

"I'm sorry I let you down, sir," Alan finally said, "but if it was any other finalist standing here naked in this living room, you would give me another chance. You know it and I know it." Then Alan looked at Bree, a look of pure hatred on his face, and then he left, slamming the door behind him.

As soon as the door slammed shut, Robert's already drained body seemed near collapse. He kept his hand on Bree's arm, escorting her, as he walked toward the condo's sofa. When he sat down, he sat her down on his lap, her body straddling his to where she was facing him.

Bree didn't know how to react to this. She knew he was angry, and should have simply let her go, but for some reason he seemed determined to keep her right here with him. For a long few moments he didn't say anything, as her body sat on top of him without him putting his arms around her as she would have expected if he wasn't upset. But he was highly upset.

"You wanted a job that badly?" he finally asked her, his intense eyes staring unblinkingly into hers.

"I needed it badly, yes. But that's not why I agreed."

"Nonsense!" Robert roared, his anger now unleashed. "You didn't need anything bad enough that you had to lose your self-respect to get it! You *wanted* it badly, that's what this is about. Wants, not needs! Like every ambitious, do-anything-to-win scum of the earth, you wanted this! So don't you dare sit here in my face playing the martyr now. I know the game, lady. I've been played more times by better scam artists than you, I know this game!"

"I'm not playing any game," Bree said, deciding to defend the indefensible, but seeing where she had no choice. What she had done was bad, but it wasn't because of any blind ambition the way he thought. "I found out that my father's house was in foreclosure and is going to be auctioned off in a matter of days. I wasn't going to sit by and let that happen, not after he worked his entire life to own that little house. I needed that signing bonus to help my family."

She'd told the truth and she felt she had told it as succinctly as she could, but to her surprise, Robert was unconvinced. "Is that supposed to explain everything? The fact that you had additional reasons for doing what you did? Am I supposed to be impressed by that?"

"I was just trying to tell you—"

"That you had sex with the man who would decide who won the prize, that's what you're telling me. I'm sure your family does need that money. I could fill the Chicago telephone book with families who need that money! But because they need it, and can rob a bank and steal it, doesn't mean they go out and rob a bank. And you know why they don't just go out and take it? Because they know that there are

141

consequences." He looked at her unblinkingly. "There are always consequences."

Bree closed her eyes and opened them back up again, the emotion of the moment making her too weary to want to fight anymore. "I didn't sleep with him," she said halfheartedly.

"Why? Because I showed up? Because you heard me unlocking the door?"

Bree stared at him. "Because I changed my mind."

"Oh, did you now? You changed your mind. What, while lying naked in bed you got religion all of a sudden, your morality came back? Is that what happened?"

Bree, now angry too, moved to get off of his lap, but he slammed her back down. "We haven't finished our conversation," he said equally angry. "Alan DeFrame. You wanted that gotdamn job so bad that you'd prostitute yourself to Alan DeFrame?"

"I told you it wasn't about the job."

"Oh, no, I forgot. It was about the money. The gotdamn signing bonus! So what, Brianna," Robert said, unzipping his pants, "how much will you give it up for if I want some? Hun?" He pulled out his penis and flapped open his suit coat that hung on her, revealing her womanhood. "How much will it cost me to fuck you right here and right now? Tell me, Brianna. Tell me how much I will have to pay you to do this!" He rammed his penis inside of her. Rammed it in and then stopped, as tears began to appear in his eyes. Tears were already in hers. He leaned his forehead against hers.

"Oh, *Brianna*," he said. "Why didn't you contact me?"

"I tried," Bree said, tears falling freely now. "I tried every way I knew how. But nobody would give you the message, and you wouldn't call me." She said this with some degree of bitterness, remembering how hard she tried to get a message to him. "And the way they were talking, you were expected to be in DC for weeks if not months longer. My family couldn't wait that long."

And they just sat there. It was true, Robert had every intention of being in DC far longer, but the VP was granted bail, and he wanted time to spend with his family, to explain the situation to them. In a few more days, he'd be back in DC, back plotting a defense, but he came back to take a break, too. The only reason he came by the condo, which was a block from the office, was to catch a nap before a meeting at the office he had set for later tonight. And to think what could have happened, what that asshole Alan DeFrame could have done. His heart ached with the possibilities of any other man so much as thinking about penetrating Bree, of resting inside of her the way he was doing at this very moment.

He should have called her, he thought, unable to ease the pain. But she had already told him no, that getting together wasn't a good idea. What was he supposed to do?

When he was reasonably sure that his teary eyes had cleared up, he sat erect and looked at Bree. And slid his penis out of her. "It's getting late," he said. "You'd better get going."

Bree felt as if this day couldn't possibly get any worst. She got off of his lap and went over to her clothes and dressed. She walked back around to the sofa, and handed him his suit coat.

"I didn't sleep with Alan," she said again, to be clear, although it sounded a lot like doing marijuana, but claiming to not inhale. The fact that she had decided to do the deed at all, instead of backing out of it later, was perhaps the greater sin.

When it was apparent that Robert had nothing more to add, and they both were spent and pretty well done with each other, Bree walked over to the front door, looked back at him once again, and left.

The next morning, eleven finalists set at the table in the twenty-first floor board room and waited to hear the news. Everybody was on edge, as if they all thought they actually stood a chance, with some eyes trained on the door that led to Alan DeFrame's office. They had not, apparently, heard the news. But as soon as the board room door opened, and Monty Ross rather than Alan entered, the electricity that filled the air was tangible.

Monty was surprised when he did not see Bree among them. He even asked why.

"She packed up and left last night," Prudence said, with some relish.

"And where exactly did she go?" Monty asked.

"Mississippi," Deidra said. "Where else?"

Monty hated to hear that. But with Alan's firing and Robert's awful mood, he had a pretty good idea what might have transpired. He therefore got on with it, and didn't mince words.

"Mr. Colgate and I will be heading back to DC in the next few days. However, he asked me to personally thank each and every one of you for your interest in working at Colgate and your devotion to the program."

Pru's hand flew up in the air. "Excuse me, sir, but may I ask, where's Alan?"

Monty cleared his throat. "Mr. DeFrame is no longer with Colgate," he said to gasps of astonishment. "Yes, well, in any event, I just want to personally thank each and every one of you for your fine contribution. I'm certain you learned a lot, and we certainly have gained a lot by having you on board. I just wanted to let you know that Colgate appreciates the contribution each one of you has given to this effort. There can be only one winner, but in my book you are all victorious. However, a winner must be selected and Mr. Colgate has selected one. Prudence Cameron is our winner," he said, and Prudence grinned. "Congratulations, Pru."

Although the entire room applauded and congratulated Pru also, Deidra sat in stunned silence. She could hardly believe her ears. Alan had guaranteed her, and he had guaranteed her repeatedly, every time she slept with him. Now Pru was the winner? Prudish Pru? And what was all of this about Alan no longer with Colgate? And why did Bree all of a sudden skip town? Deidra smelled rat in this stew. And she would use every resource her family had available, including a lawsuit if necessary, to carve out that rat, and, ultimately, bring that snob Robert Colgate down. Who did they think they were dealing with? She was Deidra Dentry. Her grandfather was once a justice on the United States Supreme Court! If she wasn't allowed to be here, the granddaughter of a judge, nobody was going to be here. And as she looked at Pru, the girl who perpetually pats herself on the back, she wondered what in the world were they thinking? What in the world was going on? She looked to Monty.

But he had nothing further to add. He thanked them again, instructed them that they will receive awards of merit for their service, and that was that.

But Deidra was steaming. *That* was a long way from *that*, as far as she was concerned. And Alan DeFrame would not hear the end of it, nor would Colgate, and nor would that Prudish Pru. When she got through with them they'd rue the day they ever heard of her. Because *that*, she thought as she packed up to leave the building for good, was nowhere near what they thought it was going to be.

TEN

"It's never easy, is it?" Malcolm asked and looked at Bree.

Bree drained down more of her bottled Coke and didn't respond. The fact that she had gone to every possible place around Nodash and surrounding towns that were hiring attorneys, and turned up empty, already proved his question. "This sucks," she said instead.

They were on the porch of her family home, sipping Coke in the warm, late-afternoon heat. Bree, a dark pair of sunglasses covering her eyes, wore a pastel-colored sundress that looked simply divine to Malcolm, while he wore jeans and a navy blue Ole Miss t-shirt. Every time he saw Bree again he regretted his decision to dump her, because he really hadn't found an adequate replacement, but he was always a man who kept his word.

"You can always go further south, to Jackson, or even Hattiesburg."

"I know," Bree said, looking out at her three younger siblings, who were playing kickball in the front yard, "and I will, I won't have any choice. It's just that I was hoping for something like right away."

"To save the house."

"Right."

"You ain't gonna find that kind of money around here, Bree, even if you do get a job right away. Not no forty-thousand dollars."

"Forty-two thousand, to be precise." She looked at Malcolm. "I was hoping to get some kind of advance, and try to bid on the house myself at auction. Jerlene," she yelled to her eight-year-old sister, "stop throwing that ball like that or you can take your behind in the house right now."

"They be throwing it hard at me," the pint-sized Jerlene yelled back.

"You heard me," Bree warned.

"I still can't believe your mama did that," Malcolm said. "And while your father was on his dying bed."

"Yeah, well," Bree said, sipping more Coke, "believe it. It's done now."

"If you ask me you should just let her lose it. Maybe she'll learn her lesson then."

"And my five younger siblings will be homeless until I can get a job and find a place to stay. Yeah, Mal, that's a real solution." Then Bree exhaled. "Sorry," she said. "I'm just fed up, that's all."

Malcolm stared at Bree. "What happened in Chicago?" he asked her.

Bree looked at him, wondering if he had heard something, but realized it would be an impossibility. "Nothing happened, what do you mean?"

"You don't talk about it? You wasn't hired, that's obvious, but you said just being selected was a victory in and of itself. But it's a funny thing: you don't seem victorious at all. In fact, you seem downright defeated."

If he only knew, Bree thought. "I'm just . . . disappointed, that's all. And I don't like to talk about my disappointments."

"Your mama said something about you having a sugar daddy while you were there, and that's how you got up her bail money."

Bree snorted. "Believe that if you want."

"But you did get up that ten thousand awfully quickly."

"Yes, I was able to borrow it."

"Couldn't you borrow--?"

"No," Bree said quickly, definitively.

Malcolm stared at her longer, deciding that she'd changed since she went to Chicago and he wasn't altogether sure if he liked that kind of change in her. But he didn't dwell on it. He sipped his Coke.

A silver sports Mercedes drove onto Rooney Street and stopped at the curb in front of the Hudson residence. Malcolm was the first to see the visitor, and then the children.

"Looks like you got company," he said.

Bree looked too. When Robert stepped out of the car, in his tan sports coat and khaki pants, and began walking toward the porch, her breath caught.

"Wait a minute," Malcolm said, shocked. "Isn't that. . . that looks like. . . Isn't that *Robert Colgate*? But it can't be!"

While Malcolm was in a conversation with himself, Bree was staring at Robert. Because she knew it could be. Even Jerlene ran up to the porch rail.

"A white man coming," she alerted her big sister.

Bree almost rolled her eyes. "Yes, I can see that," she said.

Jerlene and the other children stared at the novelty of it, as Robert walked toward the porch, but children being children the novelty quickly rubbed off and they continued their kickball game.

Robert, however, found the entire scene more enchanting than novel. A poorly paved southern street filled with pecan trees, magnolias, and bushy hop trees; small but neat frame houses; little children running around kicking what looked like a beach ball, and Bree.

She was seated on the porch, looking stunning in the prettiest sundress, her spaghetti straps revealing her small but muscular deep-toned arms, that oh-so-smooth neck of hers, and the fullness of her sizeable breasts. He also saw, however, that she wasn't alone, but was sitting and talking with a very attractive young man.

His heart began to hammer as he approached her. It was ridiculous really. He was Robert

Colgate, a man considered to be the best criminal defense attorney of his generation, a man handpicked to defend the former Vice President of the United States for crying out loud, and he was nervous about seeing young Bree Hudson? But it was a fact. He was nervous as hell.

Malcolm wasn't nervous, but he was shocked as hell. "Are my eyes deceiving me, Bree," he asked her, "or is that Robert Colgate, THE Robert Colgate, walking up this very driveway on this Rooney Street in this Nodash, Mississippi?"

Bree would have smiled at the way Malcolm phrased that, if she wasn't so jittery herself. "Yes," was all she could manage to say.

"Hello, Brianna," Robert said as he walked up the steps.

"Hi," she said, unsure what else to say.

Robert's bright blue eyes, however, immediately moved to Malcolm as he approached them. Malcolm, still stunned, stood up.

"Robert, this is Malcolm Burgess. Malcolm, Robert Colgate."

"Hello," Malcolm said, shaking Robert's hand.

"Hello, Malcolm, how are you?"

"I'm . . . shocked, actually," Malcolm admitted. "Never in a million years would I have expected to see Robert Colgate in Nodash, Mississippi. Let alone at Bree's house."

"Quite frankly," Robert admitted with what Malcolm could only describe as a grim look, "neither would I. But it was Bree and I had a few days off. Why the hell not?"

"That's right, you're defending our illustrious former vice president against rape allegations."

"Correct."

Malcolm shook his head. Bree braced herself for a confrontation.

"I take it you do not approve, Mr. Burgess," Robert said.

"Of you defending him? Of course I approve."

"Malcolm's a civil rights attorney," Bree said, hoping not only to simply point that out, but to steer the conversation away from hostilities. It didn't work.

Malcolm kept on. "But you'd better believe I don't approve of the fact that a former vice president would even dream of having consensual sex with a hotel maid. Because that's his defense, right? That the sex was consensual? That he checked into the hotel and they both agreed to have a roll in the hay? Well I say that's a load of bullocks! How in the world could a lowly maid trying to keep her job, trying to provide for her poor family, turn down Jason Bradford, the former Vice President of the United States? There's nothing consensual about it, Mr. Colgate, and that's only if it was consensual, which, in my view, is a mighty big if."

Bree could tell Robert didn't like Malcolm's assertions. But instead of battling with a civil rights attorney whose mind was obviously already made up, he looked at Bree.

"May I sit down?" he asked her. *Before I fall down with exhaustion*, he wanted to add.

"Yes, of course," Bree said, sliding over on her swing seat. Although it was a seat built for two, it wasn't exactly roomy and Robert wasn't exactly skinny. That was why, when he sat beside her, their bodies had no choice but to touch. For Robert it was perfect, as he placed his arm over the back of the seat, effectively staking some demonstrative claim to Bree. For Bree, however, their closeness was too unexpected for her to find it anything but unsettling.

Malcolm, whose chair was almost in front of, but slightly more parallel to them, sat back down. As soon as he did, a burst of laughter went out from the front yard as one of the children fell on her rump.

"Your siblings I take it," Robert said with a smile.

"Three of them. The other two, Candy and TT, are over to their friends' houses. You know how teenagers can be."

Malcolm, a master at seizing the moment, saw an opening and took it. "Do you have any children, Mr. Colgate?" he asked, and Bree was mortified. Not because of the question, it was a simple question, but because she had never thought to ask it herself.

"I have a son, yes," Robert said, to Bree's shock. Somehow she had never equated Robert with children.

"Boy or girl?" Malcolm wanted to know.

"Boy. He's in college."

"Ah," Malcolm said, noticing Bree's discomfort, but caring about her too much to see her unnecessarily hurt by a man like this, a man he already had heard was a womanizer. "So you're married?"

"No," Robert said, knowing where this was leading, and therefore deciding to be clear. "I've never married."

"You never married the mother of your son?"

Bree could tell that Robert didn't like the question, that he felt Malcolm was digging a little too deep with that one. "No," he said in a voice that bespoke finality.

Malcolm smiled. Mr. Colgate was easily riled, he thought. Which meant he had pushed a button. But he let it slide, for Bree's sake, but in so doing he created a vacuum of silence in the conversation.

Robert, for his part, looked at Bree as the threesome sat silently, at her curvy legs crossed with her feet pointed downward in a ballerina pose, at the bottle of half-consumed Coke in her hand, at her face. He lingered on her always interesting face. "You left early," he said into the silence.

Bree really didn't want to discuss the most shameful episode of her life in front of Malcolm, or anybody else for that matter, but Robert's stare would not relent. "Yes," she said. "I didn't see the point in staying."

"You stay to complete what you started." Her sunglasses were annoying him. He wanted to see her gorgeous eyes.

Bree looked at him through the dark tint of those glasses. "Did you select me?" she asked pointblank.

Robert hesitated. She'd never know how hard he battled with that very decision. "No," he said.

Bree looked away from him, the idea of working so hard, making a monumental mistake, and then turning up blanks still painful to her. "Well then," she said. "What would have been the point?"

"The point," Robert said, "was that we still had unfinished business."

Bree immediately glanced at Malcolm when Robert spoke so personally. She was mortified. She didn't want her personal business on display like this. Malcolm, knowing Bree well enough to understand that, stood. Although the idea of his Bree with Robert Colgate was still weirding him out.

"I'd better take off," he said as he stood. "Take care of yourself, Bree."

"You, too, Mal, and thanks for putting in that word for me at your firm."

"I'm just sorry it didn't work out."

"I know. But thanks."

"Maybe we can catch a dinner and movie or something once you get settled in." Malcolm could see Colgate didn't like even the suggestion of him going anywhere with Bree, which only made it clearer to him that that sugar daddy Francine was claiming Bree had in Chicago, despite Bree's denial, was Robert Colgate himself.

"Sure," Bree said with a smile. "I'll like that." Although Malcolm had dumped up as a girlfriend, he still remained her closest friend.

"Mr. Colgate," Malcolm said, extending his hand. Robert stood up and shook it. "Nice meeting you."

"Same here."

"And as for defending the VP," Malcolm said, a smirk already on his face, "good luck with that."

Robert smiled. "Just stay away from my jury pool," he said and Malcolm laughed.

"Have a good one," Malcolm said as he headed down the steps toward his Ford Taurus, the children all stopping their play and walking him to his car. What Bree always loved about Malcolm was his lack of pretentiousness, the fact that he practiced what he preached.

As soon as Robert sat back down, however, that unpretentious young Malcolm became the hot topic of their conversation. "And you know him how?" Robert wanted to know.

"I've known him for years. We sort of grew up together. Then we went to law school together. That's when we really became friends."

"Only friends?"

Bree looked at Robert. "Excuse me?"

"You heard me. Were you and Mr. Burgess only friends?"

"We are now."

"And back then?"

"Robert, I really don't see what this has to do with--"

"It's a simple question, Brianna. Were you and Mr. Burgess only friends back in your college days?"

Bree smiled. "You talk as if they were years ago. I only just graduated four months ago, remember?"

"My point entirely. And those months before you graduated, which, as you point out, weren't all that long ago, were you and Mr. Burgess only friends then?"

What was the use, Bree thought. "No. We were lovers. All right?"

Robert's heart sank. And now she was back, he thought, to continue to love affair. "But you say not any longer?"

"He dumped me in our last year at law school. Said I just didn't make the grade for the kind of wife he would require."

Robert looked at her. "And what kind of wife did he require?"

"A housewife," she said without hesitation.

Robert smiled, and then laughed. "I see," he said.

"What's so funny?" Bree wanted to know.

"I would have to agree with young Burgess. I can't see you in that housewife role."

Bree smiled and put her Coke up to her mouth. "Me either," she admitted.

Robert's arm on the back of the seat curved to where his hand was now touching Bree's bare upper arm. Bree immediately felt the heat when he touched her.

"I've been thinking about you," he said. "About us."

Bree didn't know if she wanted to have this conversation, especially not after what had happened the other night and the compromising position he had caught her in. "What about us?" she asked him.

Robert began to rub her upper arm. "I've had so much on my plate lately," he said. "I feel like I've been neglectful."

Bree found herself leaning into his rub. "How could you neglect me when we already had decided not to pursue anything?"

"Correction, my dear," Robert whispered in her ear. "You had decided that. I hadn't decided a thing."

Bree looked at him. She wasn't about to get hopeful, not after the other night, not after her own decision to not go down that relationship road with him. But she needed him to be clear. "So what are you saying?" she asked.

He hesitated, which, to Bree, wasn't exactly the sign of a man with a plan. "I was very angry with you when I saw you in that condo with DeFrame." Bree's heart dropped. "I was so angry that I had considered kicking you out of the program right then and there, without even allowing you to show up for the last day."

"We, Alan and me, didn't do anything."

"I know that," he said. When he had put his penis inside of her that night, and felt that wondrously juicy warmth that only she could make him feel, somehow he knew instinctively that no one else had penetrated her since the last time he had that privilege. And somehow he also instinctively knew that no one else ever would. "But I couldn't get past the fact that you had considered it. That you had allowed yourself to even dream of it."

Anger and defensiveness overtook Bree and she quickly snatched his hand from her arm and stood to her feet. She at first thought to pace the porch, but thought again and leaned against the porch rail, her siblings and their friends arguing over a call and not even noticing her agitation. She stared at Robert. "What do you expect from me?" she asked him, a frown of anger and confusion and regret piercing her face. "Hun? Some kind of perfection? I'm supposed to be some angel or something? My mother was about to lose a home my father had entrusted to me, to keep his children safe, to keep his children from begging in the streets or depending on any government anything, and hell yeah I was desperate! I needed forty-two thousand and I needed it within days and Alan was dangling fifty. So yes I decided to take it. I wasn't willing to let my younger siblings go homeless to prove some point. So judge me all you please, but I did what I had to do."

"But you changed your mind," Robert said, studying her, pleased with her passion.

Bree just stood there. "Yes," she said. "I changed my mind."

Robert stood up, walked over by the rail, and leaned against it too, folding his arms. "And nothing's changed regarding your family home," he said.

Bree frowned, looked down, the mere thought of what was to transpire in a matter of days weighing heavily on her. "No. Nothing's changed."

Robert exhaled. Then he reached into his breast pocket, pulled out an envelope, and handed it to Bree.

"What is it?" she asked him.

"Open it and see."

Bree opened the envelope. To her shock, it was the deed to her father's home, a deed that showed paid in full and Brianna Hudson's name as sole owner. She looked at Robert. Stunned speechless.

"Now that you don't have to worry about any roof over your siblings head," he said, "I want you back in Chicago with me."

"But . . . You paid it off?"

Robert smiled. He thought they were beyond that obvious point. "That's correct."

"But. . . but why? I thought you said you were so angry with me, so disappointed in me?"

"And in that anger, in that disappointment, I realized a simple truth, Brianna." He looked at her, found it too impersonal. He therefore took it upon himself to remove her sunglasses off of her beautiful eyes, eyes that radiated a soft glow against the natural light. He then put his hand on the banister behind her, effectively locking her into his space. "I realized that I didn't want to, that I couldn't live without you. And that kind of reality, that kind of love, Brianna, can't be shaken by doing nothing."

As soon as he said it, as soon as he so much as mentioned the word love, Bree fell into his arms. She didn't care that her siblings were now watching, and were laughing and pointing as if they'd never seen anything like it. She didn't care that her mother had come to the screen door wondering what all the fuss was about, only to see her daughter locked in an embrace with some white man driving some fancy Mercedes. She didn't even care that what she was doing went completely against all of her prior big talk, about not being ready for any hot and heavy romance with Robert, about not falling into any one-sided relationship. She just didn't care. All she cared about, at this moment in time, was the man who held her so lovingly in his arms, who rescued her family from certain catastrophe, who judged her just as harshly as she had judged herself, but regained his faith in her. And a man like that, as her father once said about something totally unrelated, *don't grow on no trees*.

ELEVEN

The rain beat heavily against the window pane as Bree lay in her childhood bedroom and watched the stars through the curtain-less frame. Robert had taken her to dinner, to the Nodash Flip and Dip of all places, and Bree couldn't help but laugh at the big man sitting in such a down home establishment, especially when the waitress said that they served grits all day and a puzzled look crossed Robert's gorgeous face.

What she mostly loved about the night, however, was that he didn't pressure her. He didn't even suggest they get a room or anything like that. He drove her back home, told her he would give her overnight to think about his offer, and that he'd stay overnight at the Days Inn, the only decent motel in town, awaiting her response. But it was the offer itself that was keeping Bree awake.

He told her about it when their plates arrived and the waitress, a seductress from way back named KatyMae, finally left them alone. He wanted to hire her as an attorney at Colgate, where she would occasionally try cases, but mainly she would run the recruiting program Alan used to run. It would give her a higher rank than any other starting attorney and would more than provide her with the standard of living she would need to provide for herself and her siblings. It sounded so wonderful to Bree that she could hardly believe it. And, once again, her father's voice told her it sounded too wonderful. "What's the catch?" she could hear him asking.

"What's the catch?" she asked Robert.

Robert was staring at his plate of chicken and dumplings, fried okra, and red beans and rice as if it were a plate of worms. "No catch," he said without looking up, his fork and knife poised to dig in.

"Then what you're saying is that this job offer is just that, a job offer, and I can live anywhere I want to live and date anybody I want to date, right?

Robert tasted a dumpling, found that he liked it. "I don't understand what you mean. Why would you be dating somebody else, and of course you can live anywhere you want to live."

"I'm just saying."

"I'm offering you the job because I believe you can do it and do it well. Now if you're suggesting that my offer implies the fact that I want you in Chicago with me, then you're correct. I want you in Chicago with me. I'm not making a secret of that."

Bree's heart began to pound. "But what do you want me to do in Chicago with you?"

Robert considered her. "I want you and me to see if we can make it work. A relationship that is."

Their eyes met. Bree held his gaze. "A long term relationship?"

"Hopefully, yes."

"Were you once hopeful of a long term relationship with your son's mother?" She didn't think she'd have the nerve to ask it, but she was glad she did.

Robert took another heap of food into his mouth and then sat back and chewed it up. Then he exhaled. "Yes, of course I was."

"What's her name?"

"Why in the world are we discussing her?"

"You never mentioned her, nor your son, so it kind of caught me by surprise. I never read that you had a son. What's her name?"

Robert hesitated only slightly. "Sylvia," he said.

Bree stared into her glass of juice. That name just sings, she thought. "Was she beautiful?"

"Yes, very," Robert said so quickly that Bree, surprised, looked up at him. "And still is," he added. "But what does that have to do with your job offer?"

"Does she live in Chicago?"

"No, Brianna, she does not. Am I currently seeing her? No. We haven't been in a relationship in years."

"But you've seen her since the breakup?"

Robert hesitated. "Yes," he admitted.

"How long did you guys stay together?"

This caused another hesitation. "A decade," he admitted.

This floored Bree. She looked at him. "Ten years? You stayed with her for ten years?"

"That's right."

"For the sake of your son?" she asked hesitantly.

Robert stared at her. He could lie, but he couldn't. "No," he said.

Their eyes continued to hold each other's gaze. Until Bree finally looked away, her heart as confused as it had been the night he made love to her. And she realized that she really didn't know him at all. "Your son, what's his name?"

"Zachary. Zack."

"Colgate?"

"Yes."

Bree sat erect. Exhaled.

"We're just getting started, Brianna," Robert sought to reassure her. "Let's not rush the process. Just go home tonight and think about my offer. Quite frankly, I don't see how you can turn it down, but I'll understand if you do. You don't owe me anything for the deed to that house, or anything else. That was my gift to you, and no matter what you decide it will remain my gift to you. And if you want the job, but not me," he said with a smile that seemed laced more with anxiety than gaiety, "I'll understand that, too."

And that was all they said about it. They continued to eat in relative quiet, he took her back home, and now she was lying in bed, staring at the stars, but thinking more about him than anything else, even the dream job offer he had made to her. He wanted a relationship with her, he wanted one when she was still a trainee, and on one level just the thought of being with Robert pleased her beyond belief.

But on another level, perhaps a deeper level, it terrified her. Especially now that she knew he had a son, a son who was probably not that much younger than she was. And the fact that he had been in a ten-year relationship with his son's mother, and he still described her as "very beautiful," and yet he never married her, didn't sit well with her either. Robert seemed to her to have so many layers to him, so many pockets, that she didn't know if she wanted to take on that kind of complication, that kind of trouble.

But he looked so gorgeous today, standing on her porch, his brown hair blowing around his gorgeous face, his big, blue eyes wide with affection, his wonderfully muscular body that she couldn't keep her eyes off of. And when he said he couldn't live without her, and that he had love for her, mercy. That was something to hear from a man like him. And to offer her a dream job like the one he offered her, where she would earn major bucks, with, according to him, no strings attached, it all just didn't spell trouble to her, or anything that would really require much thought.

Then Bree smiled. Thought about her father. And she could hear him now. *Child, are you crazy? The man paid off the house, offered you a great job, said he couldn't live without yo' butt. What else you got going on? Nodash, no man, and no job? What on God's green earth is there to think about?*

But Bree did think about it. Because it couldn't just be about Robert and what Robert wanted. It had to also be about her, and what she wanted. And the longer she thought about it, the more certain she became. And by the time she had gotten out of bed, thrown on a pair of jeans and a t-shirt, grabbed her mother's keys off of her dresser and ran, through the drenching rain, and plopped down into her mother's big old Buick, her certainty was like a drug. And she was so high, and so otherworldly intoxicating, that she was driving up into the Days Inn parking lot, a fifteen minute drive to the outskirts of town, in under five minutes.

"Ninety-one won't do," Robert said into the telephone. "We need more like ninety-eight, ninety-nine percent certainty before I'll take it before a jury." He was seated on the edge of the bed, in his motel room, talking on the phone with Monty Ross. His head was bow, his eyes were closed, and he was pinching the bridge of his nose. Exhaustion couldn't describe how tired he was.

"Pete thought he had it figured out," Monty said on the phone's other end, "but I'll tell him to refigure."

"Do that."

"You know we need to meet before we head back to DC."

Don't remind me, Robert thought, and once again wondered why in the world did he agree to represent Bradford. "I know."

"Which, my sources tell me, could be as early as a day or two."

"Understood."

"So when will we be meeting? I need to give the principals enough notice."

Knocks could be heard on Robert's room door. He frowned. Who in the world could be disturbing him in Nodash, Mississippi on this kind of rainy, miserable night? "I should be back in town tomorrow," he said as he rose and walked over to the window above the air conditioning unit. He could see nothing in the black and the rain.

"Who is it?" he yelled, before opening the door.

"It's me," Bree said, "open up."

His heart leaped with joy at just the sound of her voice, and dropped through his shoe at the thought of her turning his offer down. "I'll talk to you tomorrow," Robert said into the phone, hung up, and immediately opened the door for Brianna.

She was soaking wet by the time he took her by the arm and hurried her inside.

"Bree," he said as he grabbed her and pulled her out of the rain, "what in the world are you doing out in this kind of weather?"

"I had to talk to you," Bree said, chill in her voice, her earlier adrenalin giving way to a kind of nervous reality.

Robert looked at her, looked at her fully erect nipples poking her wet t-shirt, and his manhood began to swell almost immediately. But he turned off the A/C and moved toward her.

"Let's get you out of those wet clothes," he said as he began to quickly undress her. "Before you catch your death."

Robert removed her t-shirt, revealing her braless breasts, and then he pulled down her jeans, revealing no panties. Which probably meant, he figured, she had dressed awfully fast. He hurried to the bathroom, grabbed a big, white, terrycloth towel, and hurried back into the room, drying her entire body and then wrapping her in it.

Then he stood there, holding her by the catch of that towel, and smiled. "I'm very glad to see you," he said, "but not in this kind of weather. And is that big old Buick out there your car?"

"My mm-mmother's," Bree said, still cold.

Robert lifted her into his arms, pulled back his bed covers, and laid her in bed, removing the towel and covering her up as he did. Then he went to his suitcase, grabbed a brand new dress shirt he still had in its original wrappings, torn it open, and then put the shirt on Bree.

He sat on the edge of the bed beside her prone, covered body. "That's your mother's car?"

"Yes."

"What do you drive?"

"My mother's car."

Robert smiled, although it was hardly funny. The idea that this woman, *his* woman, could be in this kind of financial state bothered him no end. He rubbed her braids, loved the way her nose twinkled when she smiled. The things he would give to her, he thought.

"You said you came all this way, in this monsoon, to talk to me?" Robert was praying that it wasn't bad news, that she hadn't decided that she didn't want to hitch her wagon to him, or even his company. But what he loved about Bree was her individuality, her ability to make decisions based on what had to be done, rather than what she would prefer. She had great leadership instincts, he thought.

"Yes," she said. "I just wanted to tell you okay."

Robert expected more. "Okay? Okay to?"

"Everything, all of it. The job offer, and the relationship offer."

Robert smiled, his heart leaping again. 'Brianna, are you sure?"

Bree nodded her head, still chilled to the bone. "I'm sure."

Robert's smile left, and just like that Bree could see his drain. "You won't regret it," he said with all seriousness. "I'll be the best man I can be to you, Bree."

"And as soon as I warm up, I'll be the best woman I can be to you."

Robert laughed, and then quickly undressed and got in bed with her, pulling her chilled body to his overheated one. And if she thought Robert would be able to just warm her up and then leave her alone, she was monumentally misinformed.

Robert held her in his arms, her body facing his, as she began to feel its warmth. "Feeling warmer?" he asked her.

"Yes," she said, snuggling closer to him. And it was that snuggle, where her butt pushed directly onto his penis, that caused him to lift the shirt she wore just enough to reveal that butt, to lift her leg, and to slide that ever-expanding penis inside of her.

Bree closed her eyes when he entered her. It was exhilarating. And as he slid in and out of her, making her feel warmer and warmer with each slide, she knew she couldn't ever give this up again.

Robert felt that way also, as he caressed her with his penis, as he eventually laid her on her stomach, eased on top of her, and began to pump her. He loved this woman. He loved everything about this woman. And the thought of it, that he was going down this road again, made him feel almost inadequate. Except he could never feel inadequate, inside of Bree.

TWELVE

A week later, on a bright Monday morning, she entered the revolving doors of the mammoth Colgate and Associates office building and hurried for the B elevators, her briefcase at her side, on her way to the tower. By the time the elevator deposited most of its riders and made its way to the tenth floor, Prudence Cameron stepped on, with a stack of documents in tow. When she saw Bree, she frowned.

"Bree?" she asked, stunned. "What are you doing here?"

"Hello, Pru," Bree said with a smile, her body leaned against the back rail. "Congratulations."

"What are you doing here, since clearly your *sleep your way to the top* strategy failed miserably and you had the good decency to leave early? Why are you back?"

Although Pru's comments stung, Bree was relieved when the elevator stopped at the twelfth floor, and more people piled on. When the doors shut again, she and Pru were too far apart to continue any conversation. And by the time everybody else who had come on were off and they were the only two left to keep traveling all the way up to the tower, Pru was reading a text on her cell phone and had apparently forgotten all about Bree.

Until they stepped off of the elevator and saw, at the end of the corridor, Robert seated behind his desk talking with three gentlemen, but not so engrossed in conversation that he couldn't see that Bree was now on the floor.

"Brianna!" he yelled from his office, causing both Bree and Pru to look his way. "Come here."

Bree smiled and headed for Robert's office. Pru frowned and walked over to Lois' desk, handing her the stack of documents in her hand.

"I see Bret Drysdale have you document dumping again this morning," Lois said.

"You know it," Pru said, then gave Lois one of those *what's up with that* looks, as her eyes drifted toward Robert's office.

"Haven't you heard? Mr. Colgate personally hired Bree to run the recruitment office." Then Lois smiled. "She's higher ranked than you, Pru. She might even be your supervisor."

Given what Pru had just said to her potential supervisor in the elevator, Pru didn't see the humor. She was too mortified by the implications.

"Come on in, Brianna," Robert said as he stood to his feet and Bree made her way into his office. The three gentlemen seated in front of his desk all rose to their feet.

"When did you get back?" Bree asked as she made her way around his desk. She arrived in Chicago yesterday afternoon and, with the key he had given her, made her way to his penthouse apartment shortly thereafter. He had asked if she would prefer her own place, but she knew she couldn't afford a Chicago apartment right now and asking him to pay for a separate residence for her, especially since she would probably spend most of her time at his place anyway, would have been ridiculous. "I thought you said you wouldn't be back in town for another few days."

"Our client needed another family break," Robert said and kissed her on the lips, his arm lovingly around her. "Settled in okay?" he asked her.

"Yes, thanks," Bree said. She found that she loved being at Robert's apartment. It was peaceful and clean and she was already able to do a little decorating of her own without feeling as if he would disapprove. When they were in Nodash they each made it perfectly clear that they were in this relationship for the long haul.

"Guys, I would like for you to meet my very special lady here, Miss Brianna Hudson. She also runs my recruitment office."

All of the men said their hellos.

"Bree, this is--"

"Oh, you don't have to introduce any of these gentlemen," Bree said with a smile, as all three were renowned attorneys in their own right. "Wade Furth, Gerald Steiner, and Lee Clayton, it's an honor to meet each one of you." Especially Lee Clayton, she thought. He was one of the most celebrated African-American attorneys in the country, a man who shouldn't be sitting second chair to anyone, not even Robert, but had apparently agreed to do so as a favor to Robert.

"And please, sit down," Bree insisted to the three lawyers, and they obliged. "You too, Robert," she added, certain that he was probably fatigued anyway.

"Monty's retrieving some info for me right now," he said to her as he sat back down, too, "but I've put him in charge of giving you a crash course on what your duties will entail." Just as he said it, Monty Ross entered the office. "Oh, Monty, good. I was just telling Bree--"

"You aren't going to believe this," Monty said, closing the office door behind him.

"What is it?" Robert asked, knowing all too well what it usually portended when Monty had that worried look on his face.

Monty hurried over to the flat screen TV that sat on the wall on the left side of the room, grabbed the remote and turned it on. He flipped channels until he came upon a press conference. To Robert's shock, to Bree's shock, Deidra Dentry, one of the former trainees, and Alan DeFrame, were at the podium, surrounded by journalists.

"And he did it repeatedly," Deidra was saying. "I kept telling him that his sexual advances were not just unwelcomed, but that they were making me extremely uncomfortable, extremely so. But Mr. Colgate still wouldn't stop."

As soon as Robert's name was mentioned as the perpetrator of her allegations, all three of the attorneys seated in front of his desk jumped to their feet. In fact, the only attorney still seated in a room filled with nothing but attorneys, was Robert himself. Bree, staring unblinkingly at the TV screen, was paralyzed where she stood.

"I started avoiding him," Deidra said as she took one finger and smooth down her long, blonde hair, her blue eyes almost glisteningly bright. "When I knew he was in the building that day, I would make sure to shadow one of the attorneys who was currently at trial and would more than likely be in the courtroom more than at Colgate. But, of course, I couldn't avoid him entirely. He is, after all, the head man, and if he wants you, he wants you. And he would call for me so often that it was becoming nerve-racking. And every time I went up to the tower and went into his office, he would start up again."

"Was it only words?" one reporter asked her. "Did he ever touch you?"

Deidra smoothed down her hair again. "Yes," she said. "In his office on his couch. He kissed me and fondled my breasts."

Bree's heart dropped. She remembered when she and Robert were on his couch, and how he kissed her and fondled her breasts, and did even more than that. But it was consensual. But what if she would not have agreed, but he kept asking her, kept insisting? It would have been harassment to her then.

Deidra called herself getting emotional, and was wiping her eyes with a handkerchief. "After that day, when he kissed and fondled me, I knew this couldn't continue. And although I knew it would probably cost me a position with Colgate and Associates, I went to my supervisor anyway."

"She came to me," Alan said, moving her over slightly from the center of the podium and taking the mike. "I was her supervisor at the time. "She told me then what had happened, that Robert Colgate was sexually harassing her and had, in fact, just kissed and fondled her."

"What did you do when she told you that?" a reporter asked him.

"I did what any good supervisor would have done and went immediately to the tower, to Mr. Colgate's office."

"Did he admit touching her?"

"I'm ashamed to say it, but yes, he did. He said she was a hot mama who wanted it, so he gave her some. He also admitted that she kept telling him no, but, according to him, her no, no really meant yes, yes. He did agree to leave her alone, however, after I insisted. But he did exact his revenge when he selected Prudence Cameron instead of Deidra here, who was far and away the best candidate for the job, as the new associate attorney in his firm. So, Deidra, Miss Dentry, has suffered a great deal here. And the thing that is so ironic to me is this: the man, who represents our former vice president in the rape of a lowly hotel maid, is himself accused of sexually harassing a female subordinate, a very young and impressionable woman, who was under his charge. Who are these rich and powerful men that they think the world has to bend to their will? Well I say the media, and the American people, shouldn't let these high and mighty so called leaders, but actually nothing more than flimflam men, get away with it yet again."

And that was the end of the press conference. And inside Robert's office nothing could be heard but the stone silence of fear. They all, and especially Bree, looked to Robert.

Robert sat behind his desk with the look of a man about to be read his last rites before execution. Then his look changed, to that familiar, *what can you do* look Bree was beginning to know so well, and he became animated again. "Monty, take Bree down to the recruitment office and give her more insight on what will be expected of her."

"Yes, sir," Monty said, pressing off the TV and heading for the door. He, above them all in the room, knew how Robert handled stress.

"Bree, I'll talk to you later," he said.

Bree wanted desperately to talk now, but by the look in his eyes, that flaming, uncompromising look, she heeded his order without debate and headed for the door, too.

"Okay, gentlemen," Robert said, "where were we? Yes, that's right, forensic scientists. Wade, I need you to assemble the five best in the world. Everything rides on the forensics and we want to be prepared. Over-prepared."

Bree and Monty closed the door behind them. But Bree's heart was still in that room.

It became a media frenzy. Bree, her legs underneath her butt, sat on Robert's sofa and flipped from cable news channel to cable news channel that night, with every channel discussing, debating, disparaging the allegations Deidra Dentry, granddaughter of a former supreme court justice, had made against the former vice president's criminal defense attorney. It was so ironic, that snake Alan DeFrame had said, that a man accused of sexual harassment himself would be defending another man accused of rape, and the media was playing up the irony as if it was already legendary.

The front door finally opened and Robert walked in. He and Bree worked very different hours, as hers was the more traditional nine to five, especially since she was just getting started and the new recruiting process wasn't due to take shape for another few months. Robert, however, always worked late into the night.

Bree didn't know if she should jump up and run to him when she heard the door open and close, or sit and play it cool. She wanted to run to him, but since this would represent their first night together in his apartment, and she didn't quite know how the dynamic would play out when he saw that she was now here and occupying his once private lair, she remain seated.

Robert saw her sitting there when he turned the corner from the foyer. She wore one of his big dress shirts and was watching the horrid cable news shows. At first, given this law suit that had just been slapped on him, he didn't know if he wanted to be bothered with Bree or anybody else. When he was particularly stressed, he usually preferred to be left alone. But he had invited her into his world, she had accepted, and his old lone wolf habits simply had to change.

"Hello Brianna," he said as he dropped his briefcase and keys on the Queen Anne side table and then moved toward the sofa.

"Hi," Bree said nervously, staring at him. "I know you're pooped."

He sat down beside her, his long legs outstretched. "What are you watching?"

"The news," she said and then clicked it off. "Nothing, in other words."

Robert smiled weakly. He really did look rundown, Bree thought.

"I put your food in the microwave," she said. "Would you like me to heat it up for you?"

"I already grabbed something, I'm okay."

This surprised Bree. "You grabbed something?" she asked, puzzled. "From where?"

"A friend of mine cooked a hot meal and bought it up to the office for me."

Bree wanted to ask if this friend was a male or a female, and then realized how ridiculous that would sound. Of course it was a woman. Besides, what man would cook another man a plate of hot food and then bring it to him? Bree already felt inadequate as his mate.

"How was your first day?"

"Other than Deidra's allegations, it was great."

Robert leaned his head back. Don't remind him about that Deidra Dentry. "Did Monty clarify some things for you?"

"Pretty much. I still have a gazillion questions, of course, but he says you guys aren't due back in DC for another couple days, so he'll still be available."

Robert nodded. "Good."

Bree stared at him. "So what's the game plan?"

Robert knew what she meant without asking for clarification. "I'm meeting with the attorneys in the morning. We'll see then. I want you at that meeting."

Bree was surprised. "Me?"

"Yes, Brianna, you. I value your opinion and I want it expressed tomorrow morning."

She was pleased beyond measure. "I'll be there," she said. "Although I still can't get over the nerve of Deidra and Alan, please. Who would need to sexually harass her when she was giving it away like free food at a company picnic?"

Robert looked at her. "So you don't believe her?"

"Believe that you sexually harassed Deidra Dentry? Of course I don't believe it, Robert. I don't think I could ever believe something like that about you." Not a man like you, she continued to think, with your kind of looks and, beyond mere looks, sexual magnetism. Deidra would have spread her legs for him even if all he did was look down the length of her. "Thank-you," he said.

"She's a liar and the truth ain't in her," Bree said jokingly, although she meant every word, "and I know Alan is a liar. I've already got the goods on him."

Robert didn't want to be reminded of that horrible night when his sweet Bree almost slept with that slime ball DeFrame, and therefore didn't bother to ask what exactly were those "goods" she supposedly had on him. "It'll all come out in the end, I'm sure," he said, instead.

"You don't seem terribly worried," Bree said, finding his reaction to such a devastating turn of events almost odd.

"All of my worrying has been placed in Jason Bradford's defense; I have just so much worrying to go around."

"The case doesn't look good?"

"No, it looks great, actually. Especially when we fully assemble all of our scientific experts."

"Then what are you worrying about?"

Robert, his head still leaned back, stared up at the ceiling, his tired blue eyes unblinking, his brown hair flapping down into his gorgeous face. At that very moment, watching him, Bree wanted to be in his big, warm, muscular arms.

"If the case is going so well," she asked again, "what are you worrying about?"

"That maid," Robert said.

Bree stared at him. "The hotel maid? The one accusing Vice President Bradford of rape?"

Robert nodded.

Bree screwed up her face. "Why would you be worried about her?"

Robert looked at Bree. When he saw recognition light up her beautiful brown eyes, he looked back up at the ceiling.

"You think the vice president did rape her," Bree said. "Don't you?"

"Consensual sex with a maid, by the former Vice President of the United States, come on," Robert said, his face showing some irritation, his body now leaning forward. "Your friend Malcolm was absolutely correct."

"Then why don't you pull out of the case?"

Robert looked back at her. "Pull out, Bree? Jason Bradford could have asked any attorney in this country to represent him, but he asked me. And you expect me to what? Just walk away from the man, because he might be guilty as sin? What the hell kind of defense attorney would I be if I walked away from every case where the alleged perp looks guilty? I'll be walking away from almost every case I try. I'll be in a perpetual state of walking away!" Then Robert exhaled, tried to calm himself down. He stared at Brianna. She looked mortified.

He leaned back and pulled her into his arms. "Oh, Bree, forgive me," he said, snuggling her against him. "I can be an ambitious asshole sometimes, I'm sorry." Then he lifted her chin up and stared into her eyes. "I've missed you so much," he said. "And after this case is over, we'll get away, okay? Just you and me, babe. I have a cabin, a veritable retreat, in the Wyoming mountains. Maybe we'll go there. Okay?"

Bree smiled. "Okay." Then she continued to gaze into his eyes. "But I still worry about you, Robert. You can't just keep pushing yourself like this, from one case of the century to the next case of the century. You've got to say no to somebody."

Robert looked up at Bree's braids. "I've had a lot of girlfriends in my life before," he said, looking back into her eyes. "But not one has ever shown any interest in me as a man. Yes, they bring me hot meals, and I know you were dying to ask if my dinner cooker was a male or female." Bree smiled. "And they call and ask how I'm doing as often as I bother to answer their phone calls.

But it's all about them. It's all about doing whatever it takes to stay in my good graces, to stay on my supposedly hot list. Well you don't give a damn about any list, Brianna, that's why I love you so much. You love me as a person, and you wonder what you can do for me. I love you as a person, and I wonder what I can do for you. That's what love is. That's why I love you."

Robert's lips were on Bree's just as he finished his last words. And Bree closed her eyes as his passionate kissing branded her as his. Every time he kissed her it felt like a new discovery, like something so special it was almost freakish. And it made her want more and more.

He pulled her onto his lap, straddle-style, with her face facing his, and continued to kiss her, his arms wrapping completely around her, rubbing her back, moaning as he kissed.

Then he moved down, from her lips to her neck, from her neck he unbuttoned his dress shirt she wore and began kissing, sucking, fondling her breasts.

Bree's entire body ached as he fondled her, and when he laid her on the sofa, and his head was between her legs, she grabbed onto the arm of the sofa and gritted her teeth. He was so expert, and so intense, that she felt as if she was going to lift off like some damn rocket. She tried to control herself, but his passion kept her from succeeding.

Robert's control was far from chaste also, as he licked and kissed her womanhood. And with every lick, and every lift up of her pliable body, Robert knew he could hold out only just so long. He therefore lifted that body into his arms and carried her to their bedroom. And that was how he saw it now. Nothing was his alone anymore, but theirs. And that fact, too, sped up his already near its breaking point control.

After laying her on the bed and undressing as quickly as he could, he was upon her, kissing her again, licking and sucking her some more. And then he entered her. He expected it to be gradual, just a little would do, but then he plummeted in, plowed in, his control no longer self-evident. He pumped and pumped, grinded and grinded, as he wanted her even beyond any reasonableness, since he already had her.

But he kept going deeper and deeper in, and she was so juicy and wet, and all he could think about was how precious she was, how much he loved her, how much she would one day be his wife.

He almost stopped pounding her, when he inwardly admitted that truth. A man who had been so badly burned before, who planned to be a lifelong bachelor, was now thinking about a wife? But it was true. Every time he saw Brianna, he couldn't see his own life without her.

Bree held onto him with a kind of happy trust as he pounded her. She loved how he made her feel. She loved the way he always touched her where she needed to be touched, and slid into every pocket that needed his glide. This man would put all other lovers to shame, she thought. How any woman could have been with him, and not kill to keep him, to keep this kind of sexual ecstasy in their lives, was a mystery to her.

And when he screamed her name as he came, and she screamed his as she reached her summit too, she knew it was now an absolute. She was head over heels, no turning back, Johnny bolt the door, in love with this man.

THIRTEEN

Bree was the last to arrive, entering Robert's office just as the gentlemen were taking their seats around the conference table. In addition to Robert and Monty, Lee Clayton, Wade Furth and Gerald Steiner were also present. And a new player, Matt Dougan, who Bree knew was one of Colgate's best civil attorneys.

"Hello, Bree," Monty said as she entered and motioned for her to come over and take a seat. "I think you know everybody here."

"Yes," Bree said as she sat down. She glanced at Robert, who was seated on the opposite side of the table. He was on his cell phone, his big body leaned back, his eyes closed as he spoke to one of his clients. He was already up and gone by the time Bree got up this morning, which astounded her given how spent he seemed after they made love, and made it repeatedly, last night. She remembered when he kissed her this morning and slapped her on her bare butt, but she couldn't recall what exactly he had said to her. He left a note, however, telling her to be to work on time, and that he would leave the keys to his car. He owned two, his silver Mercedes E-Class and an apple-red Porsche Carrera Cabriolet. He left the Porsche for Bree to drive.

"How are you this morning, Brianna?" Lee Clayton asked. He was, in many ways, a hero of

Bree's and she was elated that he had remembered her name.

"I'm doing great, Mr. Clayton, how are you?"

"'Mister' my ass," Lee said, prompting Robert to open his eyes and look at him. When he realized Lee was smiling, he closed his eyes once again. "You'd better call me Lee."

Bree laughed. "Yes, sir," she said. "I'm just still amazed that Lee Clayton is sitting here next to me."

"I know," Lee said, his famous, whimsical look, with those piercing hazel eyes against his jet-black skin, legendary in courtrooms across America, "I have that effect on beautiful young women."

"Careful, Lee," Monty said with a smile of his own, "we don't need another sexual harassment lawsuit, now do we?"

Lee laughed. "Who? Lil' old me?" Then he winked playfully at Bree, prompting Bree to laugh.

When Robert finally ended his phone call, Matt Dougan immediately took over. Although no-one bothered to point it out to Bree, it was obvious to her that Robert had selected Matt to run his defense, a move she wasn't entirely convinced was a good one. It wasn't his skill that she questioned. She understood that he was known for getting good results for his clients, she knew about his track record. But he came across to her as a little on the arrogant and lazy side, a man who relied too much on fate and not enough on hard work.

"My strategy is a simple one, Robert," Matt said. "We'll let the little lady keep having her press conferences. We'll let her continue to make the rounds on the TV talk shows; we'll let her have her fifteen minutes. And then we'll exhaust them with so many document requests, and document dumps, so many continuances and so many interrogatories, that they will settle this nonsense long before we get anywhere near going to trial."

"Settle it?" Bree blurted out in an astounded voice, and everybody turned in her direction. Her heart pounded, but she didn't back down. "Your defense strategy in a sexual harassment law suit is for Robert to settle?"

Matt looked at Bree over the top tip of his reading glasses. At first he seemed as if he was above answering the question of some girlfriend masquerading as a serious attorney. But Robert, his boss, looked at him as if he absolutely expected an answer.

"Yes," Matt finally said to Bree, "we intend to settle. That's what we do with these kinds of lawsuits."

"But Robert's innocent," Bree insisted.

"And what, my dear," Matt said, "does that have to do with the price of tea?" He was twice Bree's age and with twice as much bravado. Nobody questioned his strategy.

"It has everything to do with it. Robert can't settle. We've got to fight this."

"Fight it?"

"Yes! With everything we have."

Matt stared at Bree. "She was your competitor, wasn't she?" he asked her.

It was one of those personal questions meant to embarrass and therefore redirect the conversation. Bree glanced at Robert, expecting him to intervene and put this Matt Dougan back in his place, but Robert just sat there, as if he was fully expecting Bree to handle this on her own. "What does that have to do with the price of tea?" was the only way she could think to respond.

"You won the man," Matt said, "but perhaps only after Miss Dentry turned him down."

Bree could not believe he had said that. She stared at Robert this time, daring him to intercede. Robert was disappointed that Bree had fallen for that old legal trick of Matt's. Instead of keeping the matter on the subject at hand, she allowed herself to be steered into defensiveness. He leaned forward. "You don't approve of Matt's strategy, Brianna?" he asked, to get her back on course.

"Of course I don't," she said, more than ready to get back. "You'll have to admit guilt if you let him turn this into a settlement case."

Wade Furst rolled his eyes. "Matt knows what he's doing, Bree," he reminded her. "He was winning cases before you were even born."

"Oh, so does that mean I'm not supposed to say anything? Because he's older than me?"

"You're supposed to respect the fact that he knows what he's doing."

"I never said he didn't know what he was doing, Wade. Did you ever hear me say that? I just disagree with *what* he's doing."

"What do you suggest, Bree?" Robert asked her and everybody looked at her, too, as if they were just certain she had no good answers in her.

Bree swallowed hard. "I suggest we fight back in kind. Deidra put you on trial, you put her on trial. Don't go around digging for information on Dee, the way Matt's saying, but dig for dirt on that bitch, and nothing but dirt. That'll put an end to this frivolous lawsuit of hers faster than any interrogatory ever would."

"And that would be your strategy?" Matt said with a sneer in his voice.

"Yes," Bree said.

"Robert is representing the Vice President of the United States, correct?" Matt asked her.

"The former vice president, yes," Bree replied.

"And your strategy is for a man of his esteem to, as you put it, 'dig for dirt' on the bitch? That's your strategy?"

"Fight back is what I'm saying," Bree said. "Deidra's proud. She couldn't survive in the court of public opinion, not that arrogance female. She'll drop that lawsuit in a heartbeat if she knew Robert wasn't going to play the gentleman and simply accept her lies, and not only just accept them, but, if we do it your way, he would willingly pay her for them. We have to fight back. And I mean hard and nasty."

Matt tossed his pen on the table and leaned back in frustration.

Wade took over. "We can't do that," he said.

"Why not?" Lee Clayton asked, which gave Bree immediate hope. If Lee wasn't dismissing her assertions out of hand the way Matt was, she stood a chance.

"Because it wouldn't be dignified, Lee," Wade said, "and would be beneath the great and widely respected Robert Colgate. That's why."

Lee, however, wasn't buying what Wade and Matt were selling. "But allowing him to admit quilt in a sex harassment lawsuit," Lee said, "isn't beneath him?"

Bree smiled. She could not have said it better herself.

Matt, however, jumped back in. "There's more to it than that, Lee, and you know it," he said.

"No, I don't know it," Lee shot back. "All I know is what I hear with my own two ears. And I heard this young lady, Brianna, make what I consider to be a rationed, cogent argument. What I hear you saying is pure bullshit. It's beneath Robert to fight back on a bogus lawsuit? That's bullshit, Wade."

"There's also the question of the litigant," Matt said.

"What about the litigant?" Bree wanted to know.

"We will not besmirch the reputation of the granddaughter of a former Supreme Court justice," Matt said.

"Her reputation?" Bree asked. "What about Robert's reputation?"

"I say again," Matt said. "We will not besmirch the reputation of the granddaughter of a former Supreme Court justice. We cannot and will not sink that low. Not as long as Robert has me at the helm of his defense. What I suggest, Lee, is that you focus on the VP's criminal case, which is your expertise, and let me handle this civil matter."

Lee glanced at Bree with that *I tried* look in his piercing eyes.

"Let's just stay the course," Monty suggested, mainly to reassure and Bree and Lee. "And let Matt do what he do for now. But Robert needs to keep his focus on the VP which, I take it," Monty said, directing this part of his comment to Robert, "he has offered his continued support?"

"Yes," Robert said. "He phoned shortly after the story broke. He says I have his full support and cooperation."

"For now," Bree said. "But if we don't fight back and allow this story to keep dripping out, I guarantee you that support will be pulled."

"*You* guarantee it?" Matt asked, amazed. "Who the hell are you? I'm sorry, Robert, but this is beginning to become Kafkaesque. The insane is taking over the asylum! This slip of a girl is just out of law school and we're supposed to sit up here and take direction from her? I know she's close to you, and near and dear to your heart, but she's neither to me. If she continues to question my strategy, I will pull out of this case and let her take it over!"

"You will do exactly what I order you to do," Robert said with a tongue lash Bree had never seen in him before. She looked at Matt, expecting a comeback, or even a walk out. But neither came. He was a mighty attorney, but Robert still was his boss.

She looked back at Robert. His look, just that quickly, had softened.

"You continue to handle the civil case," he said, "and we'll see where we are after they officially file."

"They haven't filed?" Bree asked, astonished. Then, realizing how inexperienced she really was at matters of law, didn't bother for a response. Robert, however, to his credit, Bree thought, did respond anyway.

"They've made a public intent to file, but no, they haven't officially yet."

She had more questions, but she held her tongue. She would have to talk privately to Robert about this matter, especially since Matt and Wade made clear how they felt about her. As far as they were concerned, she was simply Robert's plaything, his piece on the side, with no more legal weight than a featherweight.

Since Robert's decision to make their relationship public, referring to her as his woman instead of just his employee whenever the circumstance arose, she knew that working at Colgate would carry certain professional risks for her. But it was still an eye opener. She expected the haters to hate her, those who wanted what she had. But she never dreamed in a million years that Robert's own allies, great attorneys in their own right, would be against her, too.

And it only went downhill from there because later that night, while she was in the kitchen preparing dinner for her and Robert, the front door was opened without a buzz from downstairs. Assuming it was Robert, she wiped her hands on the apron she wore and hurried for the living room to greet him. Only it wasn't Robert who was coming around the foyer, but a young man not that much older than Bree, a blonde, blue-eyed young man. And as soon as he saw Bree, this black woman in an apron, he made an assumption that would define their relationship for some time to come.

"Didn't mean to startle you," he said with a smile that could charm birds from trees. "I'm Zack Colgate, Mr. Colgate's son. You must be the help," he said, still smiling, still clever, and although Bree understood how he could have mistook her that way, it still stuck deep in her craw.

"No," she quickly recovered, "I'm Brianna Hudson. Your father's girlfriend."

And it was obvious, by the smile that suddenly left his brilliantly lit-up face, whose craw was stuck now.

FOURTEEN

Awkward could not describe how both of them felt. He, at first, just stood there, staring at her, as if he was certain there had to be some joke, some punch line that would explain this craziness. When it was clear that Bree was dead serious, and there would be no punch lines from her, he managed to rediscover his smile and hurry toward her, his backpack bouncing at his side, his hand extended as he came.

"Nice to meet you, Brianna," he said as they shook. "I hope I didn't shock you. He's probably never even mentioned my name to you."

"Yes, he's mentioned you," Bree said. But only after questioning from her friend Malcolm, she inwardly added.

This, however, seemed to surprise Zack. "Really?" he said, studying Bree. "He usually doesn't mention me to any of his females. They're usually quite surprised when I show up."

They were now within inches of each other. He was barely an inch taller than Bree, and wasn't nearly as big and muscular as his father. In fact, there was very little resemblance. Which meant, of course, that he probably looked exactly like his mother, a woman Robert still described as "very beautiful."

"Have a seat," Bree said. "What your father didn't mention was that you were coming at all. Or that you were even in town."

"That's because I didn't tell him," Zack said as he sat in the flanking chair and tossed his book bag on the floor beside it. "I never tell him when I'm coming, I just come over. It makes me feel more at home that way."

To just barge in on his father made him feel at home? It sounded odd to Bree, but that wasn't her business. "Would you like something to drink?"

"No, I'm good."

"Why don't you join me in the kitchen? I'm still cooking dinner."

"Thanks," Zack said as he stood again and followed Bree into the kitchen. She was certainly younger than any girlfriend of his father's he'd ever seen, and he'd seen dozens over the years, and this one was a black chick too? He'd never known his father to date any African-American or Hispanic or Asian or any other race of female besides white. And not just white, but blonde and blue-eyed white. What, Zack wondered, was up with this?

He took a seat at the kitchen's center island while Bree went back to checking on her baked chicken and steaming veggies.

"So, what school are you attending, Zack?" she asked him as she cooked, turning sideways from the stove to see him.

"Oxnard," he said and studied Bree's reaction. She simply nodded. He smiled. "It's a community college in California. Mom lives in Malibu, see, so I'm not that far from her."

"I see."

"I'm studying to be a dental hygienist. And don't laugh; Oxnard has one of the top five programs in the country. Mom nearly had a heart attack when I told her. She's a Stanford grad and fully expected me to follow in her footsteps. 'Oxnard,' she said. 'Are you on drugs?' And when I told her my major, forget about it. I thought she was going to have a seizure."

Bree smiled. "What about your father? Did he approve?"

"Oh, sure. I told Dad what I wanted to do and he said good for me. He supports me without batting an eye, always, and I mean he pays everything for me. I ask Mom for fifty dollars and she wants a list of what I plan to do with it."

Bree smiled, removed her veggies from the burner.

"She's so smothering like that."

"She just seems to be very concerned about you."

"And Dad isn't?" Zack snapped, to Bree's surprise. She looked at him.

She looked at him, puzzled by his sudden snappishness. "I wasn't implying--"

"My dad loves me just as much as my mother does. If not more so! What are you trying to say?"

"I wasn't trying to say anything. I was just suggesting that your mother's concerned about you, that's all I said and that's all I was trying to say."

Zack settled back down. And although he attempted to smile off his out-of-nowhere aggression, Bree could still see the chill behind that smile. "Yeah, I tend to start and stop a lot, and that's probably why she's so smothering. This dental hygienist thing is my fourth major, if you can believe it, and Oxnard is my fourth college. I started school when I was eighteen. Normal time to start college, right? Only now I'm twenty and still floundering. I'm really a loser in the long run, I'm telling you, a big fat zero. And I guess Mom knows it."

That boy has issues, Bree thought, looking at him. But she also knew not to so much as give even encouragement. He'd snapped her head off once. She wasn't giving him a second chance.

"You went to college?" he asked her when it was clear she wasn't going to respond to his attention-grabbing 'loser' line.

"Yes. I haven't too long ago graduated law school, in fact."

Zack was amazed. "Law school? *You*?" Then he attempted to hide his disgust with yet another one of his winning smiles. "But you look my age!"

"I'm twenty-five, almost twenty-six. So I've got a few years on you."

"A very few," Zack noted. "And Dad has tons on both of us."

Bree frowned. "Your father isn't even forty yet. You make him sound ancient."

"He's just about forty, and he is ancient. Compared to us."

Bree didn't care to be lumped into any category with this kid, but she held her tongue. And within seconds, she and Zack could hear the apartment door unlock. And although she was relieved to know that Robert was home and coming to her rescue, Zack seemed suddenly nervous.

"Brianna!" Robert yelled.

"We're in here!" Bree yelled back with a smile. "He's going to be so surprised," she said to Zack.

"We?" they could hear Robert say as he headed for the kitchen. When he entered, and saw his son, he stopped in his tracks.

Zack, to Bree's surprise, jumped from the stool and ran into his father's arms. Robert staggered back by the impact of his son's embrace. For some reason Bree didn't picture Zack Colgate as the thrilled-to-see-his-parent type. To her, he was more of the spoiled, rich, *my family blows* kind of kid.

Robert had to release himself from his son's tight embrace. Not that it was difficult. Zack was now and had always been very small of frame. When Robert saw tears in his bright, blue eyes, however, his heart melted. "It's going to be all right, Zackary, you hear me?"

"What that girl said," Zack asked, "what she's saying all over TV, it's not true, Dad, is it?"

Robert rubbed his son's small shoulders. "No, son, it's not true."

"You wouldn't sexually harass anybody."

"No, I wouldn't."

"Mom says any man's capable of anything if the right woman comes along, but I told him not you. You've got all the women you could ever want. You don't have to beg anybody for sex."

Robert glanced at Bree when Zack mentioned all of his supposed women, but Bree pretended to be reading the newspaper on the island counter. Although she heard every word.

"How's your mother?" Robert asked as he moved away from Zack and headed toward Bree.

"She's great," Zack said, already feeling that emptiness he always felt whenever he was not near his father.

"Hello babe," Robert said to Bree and kissed her on the lips.

Zack's jaw tightened when Robert kissed her. "She's gorgeous as ever," Zack said. "The queen of Malibu, they call her. She's still a very sought-after supermodel, you know, despite her age."

Supermodel, Bree thought. Robert's ex is a *supermodel*?

Robert smiled. "You make her sound as if she's ready for Medicare, Zackary."

"Well," Zack said with a smile of his own as he moved back to his seat at the center island, "you know what I mean."

"When was the last time you phoned her?" Robert asked, one hand on the small of Bree's back, the other hand resting on the countertop. Bree also noticed that he was leaned against her too, as if his overworked body needed the added support.

"Let me see," Zack was thinking, "the last time I contacted her?"

"She phoned me the other night," Robert said, "and mentioned that you haven't been in touch with her the way she'd like."

She phoned Robert the other night? Bree had assumed Robert had no relationship with his ex whatsoever, that she was old news from way back. Or at least that was the way he presented it to her.

"But that's why I don't bother," Zack said. "She's always hovering, always phoning you and complaining about me. You ought to tell her to mind her own business, Dad."

"You are her business, watch your mouth."

"But you should tell her to stop calling you so much--"

"She'll call me as often as she cares to, boy, who do you think you're talking about? That's your mother you're talking about."

Bree didn't mean to show her jealousy, but she failed. Zack caught it and smiled. "You're right," he said to his father. "I forget how much she means to you, too. But she can be so . . . overbearing sometimes."

Robert realized quickly what Zack was up to. He still had foolish notions about Robert and his mother getting back together after all these years. He decided to squash all of that. "How's school?" he asked as Bree went to check on her food.

"It's okay," Zack said. "This one professor is giving me fits, but I'm used to it."

Robert tossed some nuts from a tray on the countertop. "What kind of fits?" he asked his son.

"He keeps saying my heart isn't in it, my heart isn't in it. Like what does that have to do with anything? And he just hates me, that's all. Treats me like I'm a loser."

Robert considered his son. He loved him with every breath in his body, but he was a handful. "School's still in session, isn't it?"

"Yeah, so?"

"So shouldn't you be there? Especially if this professor already has you in his crosshairs."

"Yeah, and like some horny female supposed to run around the country calling my dad a pervert and a rapist and I'm just supposed to sit in dental hygiene class and ignore it all?"

Bree removed the mitts she wore to check on her baked chicken and walked back over to the countertop, next to Robert. He continued to stare at his son, and she could tell he was worried. As if he needed something else to be worried about.

She snuggled against him, looking up into his eyes. "Would you like something to drink?" she asked him.

He smiled, touched the tip of her nose. "That would be brilliant, sweetheart, thank you."

"Wine or champagne?"

"How about both?" he said and Bree laughed. Then walked over to the wet bar.

Zack stared at her as she left, and Robert caught a glimpse of unhappiness in his son's bright eyes.

"I see you've met Brianna," he said to his son, to gauge his reaction to her.

Zack nodded. "We've met." Then he smiled. "I thought she was your maid."

Robert looked at his son. "Why would you think such a thing as that?"

"I had on an apron," Bree said from the wet bar, to make certain that no argument ensued over her.

Zack, however, grinned. "She looks like a maid, that's why I thought it," he said. "I mean she's black, she had on an apron."

"And black and apron translates into maid to you?"

Zack continued to grin. "Sure," he said, "at least that's how I see it."

"You sound like a fool," Robert said so flatly that it wiped Zack's smile off of his face. "I hope you see that, too."

Bree returned with a glass of champagne and handed it to Robert, trying her best to suppress a smile.

"I didn't mean anything by it," Zack said. "I was just joking around."

"It was a bad joke," Robert said. "And one that you will not repeat in this house. Understand?"

Zack stared at his father, his expression equal parts anger and hurt. "Yes, sir."

"This is Brianna Hudson. You can call her Brianna, or you can call her Bree. But you will not call her anything derogatory. She is my lady, my woman, my old lady, whatever is the euphemism of the day, and she will be respected with the same level of respect you accord me. Do you understand that?"

Zack was accustomed to his father's firmness, but never just for joking about one of his females, something Zack did with every female of his father's he'd ever met. But for him to get all bent out of shape over this Brianna Hudson, this black chick, was not just new to Zack, but weird as all get out.

And later that night, when Zack lay in bed in the guest room, he could hear his father fucking her in the master bedroom. And he was pounding on her the way he usually fucked his women.

Only he kept on and on with this one. On and on and on. Zack couldn't believe how long he pounded on her. And he could tell they were trying to smother their voices, but he could still hear her scream.

But when he heard his father scream out her name, as he gave her a final, full-throttle pounding, Zack's eyes flew open. Never, not in all the years he'd been going to his father's house during every summer and on weekends when he and his mother still lived in Chicago too, he'd never heard his father make a sound. He'd just do a quick-fuck on those women and send them on their way. Now he was screaming out her name? And jumping on his case for telling a nothing, innocent joke about her?

He pulled out his cell phone, called his mother. After hearing her wrath because he left school to see if his father was okay, he told her she needed to come.

"Come?" Sylvia asked into the phone. "To Chicago? Whatever for?"

"Dad's got this girlfriend---"

"Dad's always got this girlfriend. That's why we aren't together today because your father always has his girlfriends."

"But this one's different, Ma," Zack said. "She's young and beautiful--"

"Not as beautiful as I am," Sylvia said.

"No, but she's beautiful, and he treats her like he actually loves her or something."

211

"Your father? Love one of his bitches? Zackary, I know you know better than that. You sound about as believable as that witch running around talking about Robert Colgate sexually harassed her. Please. What would Robert look like harassing somebody for sex? A woman harassing him for sex would be more believable," she said with a laugh.

"It's the truth, Ma, and it's not funny. I saw him with her, the way he looks at her," he said. *The way he fucks her*, he wanted to add. "He loves her," he said, instead. Then, to really get his mother's attention, he added: "He may marry this one, Ma."

There was hesitation on the other end. Then an exhale. "Your father and I haven't been together since you were fifteen, Zack."

"But y'all still love each other, you know it and he knows it."

"I know that I still love him, yes, I know that much. He's the only man I probably will ever love. But his love for me has always been a debatable point."

"That's not true. He loves you too. He told me so."

"How long ago was that, Zack? Hun? Two, three years ago?"

"It was last year. He admitted it. He said he'll always love you. He told me so."

"But what do you want me to do?" Sylvia asked with some anguish in her voice. "I can't just run to Chicago and snatch him away from his new bit on the side. It doesn't work that way, buddy."

"Just come, Ma," Zack said. "Please. Or we may lose him forever."

Although on one level Zack knew he would never lose his father, on a deeper level, and especially with this new woman in his life, he wasn't so sure.

FIFTEEN

Monty Ross leaned back in his chair and gave Bree a knowing smile.

"So Zack's back?" he said.

"Oh, yes," Bree said, seated behind her desk, feeling slightly overwhelmed by the big office, the even bigger responsibilities, and what she was about to do. "On top of everything else."

"Don't let Zack worry you," Monty said. "Despite his angst, he's not a bad kid."

"He just plays one on TV?" Bree asked jokingly, and Monty laughed. "I can handle him," she added.

"And he'll go on and on about his mother, if he haven't already, but don't let that worry you, either, Bree. He still has this fantasy about his parents getting back together and finally getting married, which is kind of sad and pathetic really. I mean, the boy is twenty years old now, but he's still so immature. Robert told me he worries about him constantly."

"Really?" Bree asked, suddenly worried about Robert worrying so much.

"Yup. You know he had a scholarship to Stanford University, a full academic scholarship, but he decided to go to some little college somewhere just so that he could prove he was his own man? And then he flunked out of that little school, a kid with his brains? But he wouldn't do the work, wouldn't go to class, any of it. He's ridiculous really."

"Yeah, he's only five years younger than I am, but we're like light years apart in terms of maturity. He's such a kid to me. And you should have seen the way he clung to Robert when Robert came home last night. Just clung to him like a little boy. Robert had to literally force him to stop holding him. That boy has issues, I'm telling you."

"You ain't got to tell me," Monty assured her. "I already know that. Robert knows it, too, that's why he worries about him. And that's why I'm telling you to ignore him when he pulls his *my mother is this, my mother said that* routine. He loves to elevate her that way, to keep his father interested, at least in his way of thinking. To Zack, his father belongs to his mother and that's all there is to it. And he'll do everything within his power to make sure that no other woman gets any designs on his father, it's like an obsession with him. And he's going to make sure you stay in your place, too. He does that to all of Robert's---" Monty caught himself.

Bree smiled. "All of Robert's girlfriends, is that what you were going to say?"

"His former girlfriends, yes."

"So they're all former then?" Bree said this and looked at Monty. He was extremely loyal to Robert, was, in fact, Robert's best friend, but she still felt he would be straight with her, too.

"As far as I know, yes."

"And his ex, Sylvia is her name?"

"That's her."

"Is it true that she's a supermodel?"

"Oh, yes. She's a dazzler, that's for sure. She and Robert were very young when they met, but she certainly turned his head, and kept it turned for nearly a decade. Then they just kind of did their own thing. But they loved each other too much to completely call it quits. Until a few years ago when Sylvie told him she was pushing forty and wanted to get married."

Bree's heart dropped. "He wouldn't marry her?"

Monty shook his head. "Nope. Told her he wasn't interested in marrying her, the same thing he'd told her when they first met and kept telling her throughout their relationship."

"But why?"

"I don't know for sure, but I think it's because he never really trusted Sylvie. And then later in their relationship, when she wanted an open relationship, that kind of stunned him."

"According to Zack it was Robert's tail-chasing that caused his parents to finally break up."

"Oh, he did his share of tail-chasing, don't get me wrong, but that was only after Sylvie made it clear that she was already doing her own share. It was an awful time, just awful. And then she started getting bold with her shit, sleeping with men he had direct dealings with. That, to Robert, was crossing a line."

Bree's heart hammered. She nearly slept with Alan DeFrame, she nearly slept with a man Robert not only had dealings with, but had personally hired and promoted. If Monty was right, why would he trust her any more than he trusted the mother of his beloved son, a woman he had such a long history with? She was beginning to get that doubt, that sense of uncertainty as to where was her relationship with Robert actually heading. Would she end up like this Sylvia person? Pushing forty and still devoted to a man who didn't think her worthy of his name? She suddenly felt constricted.

Monty stood up. "I'd better get back to the tower. You know how that man of yours gets when I'm not close by."

"I'm worried about him, Monty. He works so hard, pushes himself too much."

"That's been Robert's way all the years I've known him. He'll be all right."

The door to Bree's office opened, and Prudence Cameron entered. Monty and Bree looked at her.

"Your secretary told me to come on in," Pru said.

"I'd better go," Monty said, "I know you've got business to take care of. Take care," he said, spoke to Pru, and was off.

Prudence Cameron walked further into the office that used to belong to Alan DeFrame but now belonged, incredibly, to her former competitor Bree Hudson, a reality Pru still couldn't handle.

"You wanted to see me?" she asked when she made her way up to Bree's massive desk. She was given an office the size of a closet, and Bree gets this suite. It wasn't fair, Pru thought.

"Have a seat," Bree said.

Pru sat down in front of the desk.

Bree leaned forward, deciding to get to the point. "Is it true that you've been telling numerous people in this building that the only reason I'm the head of the recruiting office is because I supposedly slept with Mr. Colgate?"

"Supposedly?" Pru said with a smile. "Oh, come now, Brianna. What's to suppose about it?"

"Answer my question, Miss Cameron. Are you running around this building telling people that the only reason I have this job is because of what I allegedly did with Mr. Colgate?"

"Allegedly? Here you go again. I haven't been running around doing anything. People ask my opinion and I tell it. Just like I told you to your face that you slept your way to the top, because you did. You knew Mr. Colgate liked you, for whatever reason, and you played on his favoritism. Decided to give him what he apparently wanted and he promised to give you a position with his firm."

"That is such a lie! If it was that kind of quid pro quo why didn't I get your job? Why didn't he select me after our training period, since that was my grand scheme to begin with?"

"Because that would be too obvious. Besides, he had bigger and better things in mind for you." She said this as she looked around Bree's big office, and remembered her small, pathetic one.

"I want you to stop so much as mentioning my name and Mr. Colgate's name while you work in this building, do you understand me?"

"This is a free country," Pru said. "I'll mention anything I want to mention. And since it's true, I will continue to tell the truth about you too."

"If you expect to remain at Colgate, you will stop spreading your vicious lies and you will stop right now."

Pru looked at Bree. "Who do you think you are? You can kiss my ass, that's what you can do. You're nobody, I don't care how many sleepovers you have with the top brass. You're just a poor little Negro girl from Mississippi, who attended some nothing Mississippi law school, who couldn't make it on her brains, but had to rely on what was between her legs. The difference between you and Deidra Dentry is a matter of class, you see. You spread your legs for Robert Colgate, when DeeDee wouldn't. He had to beg her for it, and still didn't get it. You, on the other hand, had a neon sign between those legs of yours. 'Come and get it,' became your battle cry and I'll continue to make sure that everybody in this building knows it, too. Telling me what I will and will not do. Who the hell do you think you are?"

"I'm your supervisor, Miss Cameron," Bree said calmly, fighting an incredible urge to slap her subordinate. "And you're fired."

Pru jumped to her feet. "What?" she asked, astounded.

Bree stood up too. "You heard me," she said. "Your little *Mississippi negro girl* supervisor has fired you."

"You can't just fire me!"

"Yes, I can, and I have. You're still on probation. As your supervisor I can fire you and fire you summarily. Which I have chosen to do. Now get your things and be out of Colgate and Associates by close of business today."

Pru was stunned. She stared at Bree as if she had suddenly grown horns. And the hatred in her eyes made Bree wince.

Pru left, slamming the door behind her.

Bree sat back down, as tears entered her eyes. She hated firing anyone, even Pru, but what could she do? Let her insubordination continue unchecked? And here she was, one of only a handful of black females in this firm and Pru and her ilk were already trying to label her as some kind of an incompetent slut. She couldn't allow that kind of cancer to remain at Colgate and spread like some kind of crazy wildfire, destroying the reputation of all of Colgate's black female employees in its wake.

It was a sister, in fact, who had called and told her what Pru was saying all over the building, and how it was affecting morale. They worked harder than everybody else to get their positions at Colgate, the sister had told her, and these rumors, these persistent, nasty rumors, weren't helpful. Weren't helpful, she had said, as if she, too, was blaming Bree.

And not an hour later, Wade Furst, Bree's direct supervisor, was in her office, to offering up his blame as well.

"Rehire her," he ordered.

"Rehire her?" Bree asked, astounded. "But why?"

"Reinstate her, Brianna. And I mean now."

"And I want to know why? You don't know what all she said to me."

"I don't care if she called you Hitler and put a swastika on your forehead, you rehire her!"

But Bree stood her ground. "No. Especially when you won't even give me a good reason why."

"Her uncle is billionaire industrialist Warren Bachmann, a man with a mighty reach at a time when we can't afford any enemies, not any. Is that a good enough reason?"

"No," Bree said. "As her supervisor that's my ruling, and my ruling is final."

Bree could see the hatred in Wade's eyes, too. "Prudence Cameron," he said with his infamous huff, "is reinstated effective immediately, and will be reassigned under a different supervisor. Consider that final ruling of yours overruled."

And he left.

Within minutes, Bree was entering Robert's office. To her surprise, Wade and Prudence were already there.

Robert, who seated behind his desk, stacks of papers in front of him, listened to all sides. Bree could tell that he didn't need or want this new wrinkle, but she didn't see where she had any choice. She wasn't letting some arrogant racist like Pru run roughshod over her or anybody else at Colgate. Not without a fight she wasn't.

"And the only reason she's firing me is because she's jealous," Pru insisted. "I was selected and she wasn't, and she can't deal with that. She never once mentioned my work product; she never once mentioned how valuable the senior attorneys regard my insight and judgment. All she harped on was the fact that I was victorious, and she was not."

"That's not true," Bree said. "Your decision to continue to spread lies and innuendo, and your blatant racism are the reasons for your termination, and you know it, Pru."

"You're lying and the truth isn't in you," Pru shot back.

"You're the one who's lying, and you're spreading your lies like a cancer--"

"All right that's enough," Robert interrupted and Bree was shocked, and disappointed, that he would interrupt her. "You two aren't going to stand up here and trade insults, at least you aren't going to do it in my office."

"Now you see how ridiculous all of this is, Bobby," Wade said. "That's why I told Bree she couldn't fire Prudence. No way, not now, and especially not for the reasons she cite."

"You didn't bother to hear my reasons," Bree pointed   out.

"It was a bunch of nonsense, that's why," Wade shot back.

"Prudence," Robert said, his face well tired of it," Brianna is not firing you."

Pru and Wade smiled. Bree's heart dropped.

"Thank-you!" Pru said, looking smug and vindicated.

"But I am," Robert added. "Pack your shit and be out of my building in the next twenty minutes." Then he looked at Wade Furst. "Wade, escort her out," he ordered.

Robert stared at Wade after he said it, as if daring him to try and overrule him. Wade's embarrassment was complete. He took a stunned Pru by the arm, and escorted her from Robert's presence.

Bree grinned. "Thanks for backing me up," she said.

Robert looked at her angrily, which confused her. "What?" she asked him.

"Did you have to do this today?"

His question threw Bree. "I . . . I just . . . What do you mean?"

"I have enough on my plate, Bree," he told her. "Don't add anything else."

"I wouldn't have added that if Pru hadn't been so insubordinate."

"You heard me."

"Yes, I heard you."

"Now get back to work."

Robert was different on the job, and Bree understood that. But it still stung. "Yes sir," she said, and left. She also knew, as she walked down the corridor away from his office, that her days as an attorney in her lover's law firm were numbered. She would see to that.

SIXTEEN

Dinner that night was filled with tension, especially when Zack sat down and was on Bree's case about firing Pru. How he even knew about it was a mystery to her.

"But it makes no sense," he said to her. "Especially now."

"So in your mind it would have made more sense later, but not now?"

"You know what I mean," Zack said. "Firing your competitor--"

"She's not my competitor."

"She was. And to fire her now, when Dad is in the middle of a sexual harassment lawsuit, makes no sense. Now she'll join forces with Deidra Dentry and create more trouble for him."

"Oh, that's nonsense."

"It's not nonsense," Zack replied, and then looked at Robert. "It's not nonsense, is it, Dad?"

Robert was seated at the table reading over a report and, quite frankly, wasn't paying either one of them much attention. "What's that?" he asked as he finally bothered to look up.

"Tell Bree she picked the absolute wrong time to fire Prudence Cameron."

Robert frowned. "What do you know about that?" he asked him.

"I've got a friend or two at Colgate who keeps me posted," Zack said with a smile. "And they agree with me too that Bree overplayed her hand."

"I didn't overplay anything. She caused herself to lose that job."

"But why now?" Zack wanted to know.

Before Bree could answer, however, Robert answered for her. "Because Brianna doesn't make moral decisions based on timing and political expediency," he said as his cell phone began to ring. "She does the right thing whether it's in season or out of season." He pulled out his cell phone to look at the caller ID. "Whether you want to hear it, or whether you don't."

"But," Zack started but Robert, seeing his Caller ID and immediately answering, put up a finger for him to hold his thought.

"Hello, Mr. Vice President," Robert said into his cell phone and Bree and Zack glanced at each other. The room was now pin-drop silent.

Bree could tell Robert was looking grave even before the call, but as the call progressed he looked even grimmer. When he finished the call and closed his cell phone, he leaned back in his chair and exhaled. Then he looked at his son and his lover.

"That was our former Vice President," he said.

"What did he want?" Zack asked nervously.

"It seems that I've been replaced as lead attorney for his defense."

Zack's fork that was in his hand slipped out. Pain appeared on Bree's face. "Did he say why?" she asked him.

Robert smiled a smile so weak that it barely penetrated his gloom. "They never say why. They just claim they're doing you a favor and leave it at that. Then I'm supposed to issue a press release stating that I'm doing the former vice president a favor, that my other legal obligations made it impossible for me to give his case the full attention it deserves and leave it at that."

"And they expect people to believe that you have other cases more important than defending the former Vice President of the United States?"

"No, they don't care if people believe it or not. They just do it. Oh well. It is what it is," Robert said in such a disappointed way that Bree, for the first time ever, felt sorry for him.

"It's all your fault," Zack said to Bree and Bree and Robert both looked at him. "If you wouldn't have fired Prudence Cameron--"

Bree frowned. "What does Pru have to do with this?"

"If you wouldn't have fired her then Warren Bachmann wouldn't have gotten to the vice president."

"Oh, that's crazy," Bree said, amazed that Zack was willing to overlook that glaring sexual harassment lawsuit that probably had everything to do with Robert being replaced.

"Who'll you calling crazy?" Zack pounced. "You're the one who's crazy! You just caused Dad to lose the best case of his career," he yelled, "you're the one who's crazy! You selfish bitch!"

As soon as the b-word sailed from Zack's lips, Robert sailed from his seat, grabbed his son by the catch of his collar and slung him against the dining room wall.

"Robert, no!" Bree yelled in fear, seeing the anger in his eyes.

"If you ever, and I mean ever," Robert said, slamming his son harder against the wall, "call Brianna anything but her name, I will kick your natural ass. You understand me?"

Zack was at this point in tears. "Yes, sir," he said.

Bree could see the regret in Robert's eyes when he realized his son probably was responding more out of love for him than disrespect of Bree. He released his son's collar, smooth it down, and then backed out.

"I need some air," Robert said as he walked toward the French double doors, opened them, and then made his way out onto the balcony to take in the fresh night breeze.

"See what you've done?' Zack said to Bree, albeit half-heartedly, as he sat back at the table.

"You are such a kid," Bree responded, "did anybody ever tell you that?"

"Oh, so because I care about my dad I'm some kind of a sissy or something?"

Bree frowned. "Who said anything about you being a sissy?"

Before Zack could respond, however, they both heard what sounded like a big fall. A hard, solid thump. They looked at each other, remembered Robert, and then ran for the balcony, with Bree leading the charge. When they ran through the French doors and saw that it was indeed Robert, that he was lying on the balcony floor, and that he was unconscious, both of their hearts dropped in a combination dread and terror.

"Lord, no," Bree said breathlessly as she hurried to Robert's side. "Call 911," she ordered Zack.

But Zack, at first, was immobile. He'd never seen his father down before, in such a vulnerable state before. Bree looked at him. "Call 911!" she yelled so loud that it woke Zack from his stupor.

And with trembling hands he dialed 911.
***
The sterile waiting room provided a relaxing antidote to the sense of chaos that both Bree and Zack felt when they saw Robert sprawled out on that balcony floor. Other than one old lady with a little girl, they were the only pair in the room. And although others came and went, three hours later and Bree and Zack were the only ones still there. According to the nurses, the doctors were still stabilizing him and running tests. His doctor, they kept saying, would be with them soon.

When the doctor finally arrived, Zack jumped to his feet. Bree, however, was too paralyzed with fear to move. She just sat on the edge of her seat as the doctor, an older man with a stethoscope around his neck, his face showing grave concern, approached.

"Hello, Zackary," he said.

"Hey, Dr. Luce, is Dad all right?"

"And you must be Rhianna?"

"Yes," Bree said, too nervous to realize that he had mispronounced her name.

"Is Dad all right?" Zack asked again. Bree didn't think it possible, considering how she felt, but Zack was even more nervous than she was.

The doctor looked at him. "He suffered a massive heart attack, Zack," he said, and Zack's already drawn face sagged even more. "He's in critical but stable condition at this point."

Bree's heart pounded. "It's bad," she said.

"Yes, it is, there's no way to sugarcoat this. But he's in excellent hands, he will receive excellent care. We expect him to have a full and complete recovery."

"Thank God," Bree said, relieved, and Zack, relieved too, sat back down.

"But he'll need to slow down," the doctor warned. "I've known Robert Colgate for darn-near twenty years and the only speed he knows is fast. That has got to change."

"It will," Bree assured him.

"Good," the doctor said, considering her.

"Is he conscious?" Zack asked. "Does he know where he is?"

"Yes, and yes. He's a strong man so he'll be fine. But he'll just have to slow down."

"Can we see him, Dr. Luce?" Zack asked.

"He's asked to see, Rhianna," the doctor said and Zack, who was about to stand up, leaned back down.

Although Bree wanted desperately to see Robert, it didn't seem right that she should usurp his son. "Let Zack go first," she said. "I'll go after him."

Zack looked at her. "You sure?"

"I'm positive," Bree said with a weak smile. "Go see your father."

Zack was taken aback by Bree's offer, but he was still too emotional about his father to turn her down. He followed the doctor out of the room.

When he returned, a few minutes later, Bree was already standing at the door ready to go.

Bree wanted to ask Zack questions, but he had that mean, contemplative look on his face that made her think the better of it. She, instead, simply moved to go.

"They said he should get his rest," Zack said when he saw her leaving.

"And?"

"And you shouldn't go bothering him right now."

"I'll be back, Zack," Bree said, not even entertaining his nonsense.

"You won't be able to see him," Zack yelled as she left.

"Watch me," Bree yelled back as she headed up the corridor to Robert's room.

Zack, now alone in the waiting area, pulled out his cell phone. Called his mother.

"Dad's had a heart attack," he said as soon as she answered.

There was a hesitation. "When?"

"A few hours ago. I tried to phone you."

"I was in makeup. How is he? Is he all right?"

"It was a massive heart attack."

"Is he all right, Zackary?"

"Yes! I guess. Dr. Luce says he will be."

"Dr. Luce? He's still practicing medicine? He must be ninety by now."

"He's barely in his sixties, Ma, what are you talking about?"

"Whatever, Zack. Have you seen him?"

"Yeah. But they wouldn't let me stay long." Then Zack hesitated. "His girlfriend is gone to see him now," he finally said.

"A heart attack at his age," Sylvia said. "He always did work too hard."

"You've got to come, Ma."

"I'll be there, you know I'll be there. As soon as I get back I'll be there."

"Get back? You're going somewhere even after news like this?"

"Listen to you. Of course I'm going. I'm due in Milan, remember? My flight leaves first thing in the morning."

"But you can cancel it."

"Cancel Milan? You must be joking! This is Fashion Week, darling. You don't cancel Milan during Fashion Week."

"Don't you care anymore about Daddy or anybody besides your stupid career?"

"Watch your tongue, young man. Of course I care about your father, I care deeply about him. But I know there's nothing I can do for him even if I did drop everything and run to be by his bedside, which he wouldn't want me to do, anyway. He knows how rare it is for a model my age to continue to get major gigs. Your father understands. Besides, he's going to be just fine."

"He asked for her," Zack said and there was a pause on the other end.

"Asked for whom?"

"Brianna. His girlfriend. He wanted to see her even before he wanted to see me. He asked for her."

"So he asked for her," Sylvia said in a dismissive tone. "That means absolutely nothing."

"It means everything, Ma. I'm telling you she's different. He sees her differently."

"Yeah, sure, until he sees me again. Then he'll forget her name. Every time we've seen each other since we called it quits, he's taken me to bed. Every single time, Zack. And it never mattered who he was dating at the time, either. I take first place every time I show up. So this Brianna person is nothing, a nobody, don't even worry about her. As soon as I get back from Milan and pay your daddy a visit, he'll forget that woman exists. And you can bet that. How much you want to bet?"

Zack didn't say it, but he'd bet against it. She didn't understand. Brianna Hudson was different. A game changer. And none of those old rules applied when playing a brand new game.

Tears flowed freely down Bree's face as she sat in a chair at Robert's bedside and held his hand. There were so many tubes going into him, so many machines beeping and bonking and squeezing in and out that she felt even worse than she had before she saw him. This was serious. This could have been catastrophic.

He slept through most of her visit, but then he finally opened his eyes, saw her face, and managed to smile.

"Hi," he said.

"Hi yourself," she said, sniffling back her tears.

"You're a sight for the sore eye."

"So are you, honey."

He touched the side of her face.

"You gave us such a scare, Robert."

"I know. Didn't mean to." He tried to smile this time, but couldn't pull it off. "I'm not a kid anymore."

"I thought, we thought we could lose you."

Robert cupped her face, considered it. She snuggled against his still big, strong, powerful hand.

Robert swallowed hard, fighting sleep, pain, and this overwhelming love he felt for Bree. "I'm not going anywhere," he said. "I don't want you and Zackary worrying about me, you understand?"

"I understand."

The nurse walked up to the bed. "He needs his rest, ma'am," she said.

"Yes, of course," Bree said, rising, wiping her tears. But Robert reached out his hand, and Bree grabbed it.

"You take care of yourself, Brianna," he said.

She nodded. "I will."

"And look out for Zack. His main crime is that he loves his old man too much." Robert managed to open his tired eyes wide again, and look directly at her. "You're strong like me. He isn't. Look out for him."

Bree smiled. "I will," she said. "Now you get some rest."

"Some of that much needed rest I've been hearing about."

"That's right," Bree said, but she didn't have to say anymore, because he was already asleep.
***

The door to Robert's apartment was opened and Bree and Zack entered as if they were entering a morgue. It was the quietness that got them. Although Robert was almost never at home, his presence still was already sorely missed.

"I'll fix something to eat," Bree said and headed for the kitchen. Zack, to her surprise, followed her.

As she pulled out food and set it on the countertop, Zack moved over to the French doors in the kitchen. Like the doors in the dining hall, these, too, led to the elongated balcony, the balcony where Robert had had his heart attack. Zack stood against the doorjamb, looking out onto the balcony, remembering the sight of his father on the floor and how much it terrified him. And the tears began to come.

Although his back was to Bree, she heard his sniffles. Robert said he wasn't a bad kid, but just that he loved his old man too much. Bree didn't know about that. Because she loved his old man even more, and she didn't consider her love as too much. But she understood his point. When you love somebody the way Bree and Zack loved Robert, anything that happens to them seeps the life right out of you.

Bree also remembered, however, how she had promised to look out for Zack, even if, was Robert's implication, he didn't want her to. She therefore set the veggies down and walked over to the doors leading out onto the balcony. She touched Zack on the shoulder. When he didn't flinch or otherwise protest, she exhaled.

"He's going to be just fine, Zack," she said, his back still turned to her, "you just wait and see. He's strong, I've never met a man as strong as your daddy, and he'll pull through this just fine. Don't worry. Please."

But the tears didn't lessen and Zack, still devastated, turned and fell into Bree's arms. Bree held him as he sobbed like a baby. "It's all right, Zack," she kept saying. "It's all right."

SEVENTEEN

Robert would spend another two weeks in the hospital, moved from ICU within a few days, and then into what they called "step down toward release" within a week. At the end of two weeks he was released and on his way, not to his Chicago penthouse apartment, but to his cabin, and considerable property, just outside of Laramie, in south eastern Wyoming. Robert had mentioned the cabin to Bree before, but when Zack told her the full details, and how he loved the peacefulness of it as a kid, the isolation, she immediately made arrangements for Robert to convalesce there.

It was like another world to Bree, as the company plane landed in Laramie and then the helicopter shuttled herself, Robert, and Zack to the cabin. Only it wasn't what she thought of when she thought of a cabin, it wasn't some square little box of a home surrounded by logs, but a beautiful brick, ranch-style home surrounded by mountain ranges in the far distant, and an open plain right in front of them. Robert, according to Zack, owned the land almost as far as their eyes could see. It was breathtaking to Bree.

Robert emerged from the helicopter looking fit as a fiddle, although if you knew him the way Bree and Zack did, you'd see that his once manic movements had slowed considerably. Stamina was the issue for him now, as he tired easily. His team of doctors, to Bree's relief, had already warned him to ease back into life with a whimper, not a bang.

And Robert had changed emotionally, too. He seemed to need Bree and Zack more than he had previous to his heart attack. He held Bree's hand, for instance, and would not release it, as they entered the beautiful home.

"Didn't I tell you it was great?" Zack asked, as excited as a kid.

Bree smiled. She and Zack had grown closer since Robert's fall, and she understood now why Robert loved him so much. "And you still didn't do it justice," she said, and Zack beamed.

Bree had hired a maid service from Laramie to clean and stock the place, and they did not disappoint. As soon as the luggage was set down in the living room, and Robert was talking with the assistant who accompanied them and would remain in a hotel in Laramie in case he was needed, Bree checked out the place. It was a beautiful, three-bedroom home with all of the amenities, except, to her surprise, a dishwasher.

She looked at Zack, who was giving her the guided tour. He smiled. "Dad thinks not having a dishwasher is roughing it."

"But a microwave is?"

"Essential, he says," Zack said and Bree laughed. Robert and his situational ethics, she thought.

***

Over the course of the next four weeks, Bree would be back and forth between Chicago and Wyoming as she was forced to begin the screening process for the upcoming new class of trainees. Robert and Zack both hated when she left, and she hated to go, but she knew, once Robert was back to normal (and he nearly already was), he'd want his business fully functioning and intact. An important component of that business was his recruitment program, and she aimed to keep it running smoothly.

During one such visit to Colgate and Associates, however, she found out from Monty that Deidra Dentry had officially filed her harassment lawsuit and was not interested in any out of court settlement, which was Matt Dougan's entire strategy. Alarmed, Bree paid a visit to Matt's office. He was a partner at Colgate, and was therefore housed in the tower not far from Robert's suite of offices.

"I don't understand what you mean," Matt said as Bree stood in front of his desk and asked about his new strategy. "Why would I have a new strategy?" He was on his feet, about to leave when she arrived, and he grabbed a stack of folders and shoved them into his briefcase.

"Deidra has officially filed her sex harassment lawsuit and has publically made clear that she's not interested in a settlement."

Matt smiled. "Public admissions aren't worth the paper their not printed on. She's just talking. She'll settle. In time."

"But what are you doing in the meantime to get this matter over with," Bree tried again. Matt was really a very arrogant bastard who seemed offended when someone even deigned to ask him a question. She once asked Robert why so many of his best attorneys were assholes. He said because they were the best. When Bree pointed out, however, that he was the absolute best, but wasn't an asshole, he smiled. Said what separated him from Matt and the other top-tier lawyers was that he understood that it was God's grace that made him great, and not some power he possessed on his own.

"You worry too much, Brianna," Matt said with a condescending smile.

"But what are you actually doing? I don't want Robert coming back with this still hanging over his head."

"I'm letting the criminal catch herself. I'm giving her the rope, and waiting for her to hang."

"In other words, you're doing nothing," Bree said pointblank.

Matt's smile left and his pretense to appreciate her concern was over. "Get out of my office," he ordered.

"But it's the truth."

"Take your gotdamn truth and get out of my office."

Bree stared at him. She wanted to fight back, but she knew she'd be pushing it. He wasn't just anybody, but was a partner at Colgate. Robert would probably kick her to the curve before he allowed her to lose an attorney the caliber of a Matt Dougan. She got out of his office.

But as soon as she made her way back into her office, she phoned Monty. "We need to meet," she said. "At Robert's house. Matt isn't doing a gotdamn thing for Robert's case and I'm not standing by and taking it another second."

"Agreed," Monty said.

"See if you can wrangle Lee Clayton."

"Ah, you want a big boy."

"The biggest that I have confidence in, yes."

"Matt won't like it."

"Good," Bree said, and hung up the phone.

***

They met around the dining table at Robert's penthouse apartment. Bree, Monty, and Lee Clayton.

"What we need," Bree said, "is dirt. Not information on Deidra, but dirt. And not just on her, either, but on her family, on that former Supreme Court justice granddaddy of hers."

"What good will that do?" Monty wanted to know and Lee rolled his eyes. Although he and Robert were friends, he and Monty barely could stomach each other. Monty saw Lee as some showboat lawyer in the spirit of a Johnnie

Cochran. Lee saw Monty as an adequate lawyer in the spirit of a yes-man to Robert.

"You don't understand what good that'll do?" Lee asked Monty.

"I'm simply asking a question," Monty said defensively.

"Deidra is a very proud girl," Bree said. "Everything she stands for is all about her virtuous family. That's what she's selling whenever she appears on these TV shows. Blonde hair, blue-eyed virtue. We've got to knock the shine off."

"But for what purpose?" Monty asked and again Lee rolled his eyes.

"The purpose is," Lee said, "that when we finish with her, she'll wish she never tussled with us."

"She'll know," Bree said, to be clearer, "that if she keeps this lawsuit going she's in for a fight. And we'll try to make her understand that with every fight nobody, not her, not her box office appealing, all-American family, will come out of this the same. If she continues to put dirt on Robert, we just want to remind her that she's going to end up with even more dirt on herself. We need all the dirt we can round up on her, and then we'll meet with her and lay it all on the line."

Monty nodded. It wasn't his style of defense, but given what Matt had in the offing with his hands-off, do-nothing approach, it would have to do.

***

Robert, in a pair of shorts and polo shirt and walking with a cane, was out on the grounds when Bree returned to his estate in Wyoming.

"Brianna!" he yelled, waving his cane, when he saw her coming up the footpath near the lake where he was standing. Although Bree had only been gone for a few days, he had missed her terribly.

"Hello stranger," he said as she approached, her jeans and silk blouse making her appear more youthful than her twenty-five years, and made him feel much older than his thirty-eight. "Made it back?"

"Yup. Glad to be back, too," she said as she stood before him. Robert had never been automatically affectionate. He first had to size you up, make sure you're okay, before he committed to any hugging and kissing. Bree even noticed how he checked out her attire, before he pulled her into his arms.

"I've missed you," he said as he held her.

"Same here."

Then he looked her in her eyes, and kissed her.

They had not had any sexual contact since Robert's attack, but she noticed just before she left how he was beginning to get that look again. Now there was no doubt in her mind as he kissed her.

But it would be another two weeks before they actually went that far. It was a breezy

Wednesday afternoon, and Bree, Robert, and Zack were relaxing on the front porch when Bree's cell phone buzzed. When she looked at the Caller ID, and realized it was Lee Clayton, she answered immediately.

"What's up?" she asked, glancing at Robert. Robert was staring at her. "

"They've agreed to a meeting," Lee said into the phone.

"That's great. When?"

"Tomorrow morning at 9am."

Bree closed her eyes. She wasn't ready to leave just yet. "Okay,' she said. "I'll see you tomorrow."

When she hung up, both Robert and his son were staring at her.

"Who was that?" Robert wanted to know.

"Lee."

"Lee Clayton?"

"Yup."

Robert studied her. "Why would Lee Clayton be calling you?" The young, smart, gorgeous Lee Clayton, he added inwardly.

"He's been helping me out, that's all."

"Helping you out? He doesn't work for Colgate. Why would he be helping you?"

"It's not related to my job at Colgate. He's just helping me out, that's all." If she told Robert what Lee was really helping her to do, he'd put an end to it instantly and let his hero Matt Dougan handle it.

"In any event," Bree continued, "I have a meeting tomorrow morning in Chicago, so I'd better book a flight online and go and get packed." She stood up. "If that's okay with you," Bree added, unsure by the look of concern on Robert's face.

"Yes, it's okay," Robert said, still staring at her.

"I'll be back."

When she entered the home, and the screen door slammed shut behind her, Zack took her seat next to his father. "Want me to go with her, Dad?" he asked.

Robert smiled, put his arm around Zack. "No, son."

"But you know how smooth Lee Clayton can be. I mean, he's a good lawyer and all, but he's a straight up womanizer."

"I know that, too. But I'd trust Brianna with my life."

"But why would he be helping her?"

Robert ran his hair through his son's thick mane of blonde hair. "I don't know. It could be personal, concerning her family."

"Why won't she just say it if that's the case? I think I should go with her, Dad."

Robert smiled weakly. "To keep an eye on her for me?"

"Yes!"

"No, son," Robert said, his smile now gone. His face grim and concerned. "I have to trust her."

Zack snuggled closer into his father's embrace and looked up at him. "You really love her, don't you?" he asked.

Robert nodded. "Yes."

"Why her? I mean, she's all right, I like Bree now, but . . . look like you could do way better than her."

"In terms of what? Looks?"

"And class and culture. You know." Zack said this with a knowing look.

"If you're trying to infer that Bree isn't some gorgeous rich white woman closer to my age, rather than yours, you're correct. She's not. She's a gorgeous woman who happens to be black, who happens to be poor, and who has agreed to love your father and give him a chance."

Zack stared at Robert. Sometimes his father was as hard to figure out as some enigma in molecular biophysics. "Her give you a chance?" he said. "Dad, I don't think you really realize how great you look and how rich you are and how any woman anywhere in this world would be thrilled to *give you a chance*, are you kidding me? She's not doing you any favors. She's probably counting her lucky stars for catching your eye."

Robert looked at his son. He still didn't understand. "You're looking at it wrong, son. It's not about what I can do for her. I know what I can do for her. But what she does for me is the difference."

Zack, however, looked doubtful. "What does she do for you?" he asked. *Other than let you fuck her brains out like there's no tomorrow*, he wanted to add. Although he had to admit he hadn't heard any such rabbit-humping from the two of them in all of the weeks they'd been in Laramie. "Well?" he asked again. "What's so great that she does for you?"

"She brings out the best in me, Zack. She makes me want to do the right thing, to live like the man I've always wanted to be, but situations never allowed me to be. In the courtroom I'm ruthless. I believe my clients, no matter how repulsive, have a constitutional right to fair and competent representation, and that's what I give to them. And I fight like a junkyard dog to get my client off."

"But you fight fair," Zack reminded him.

"I fight fair, unfair, I do what I have to do to get that favorable verdict." Robert frowned. "And I'm not proud of that. They call me the toughest attorney in America because of my tenaciousness, my win-at –all-cost mentality. But when I'm with Bree," he said, his smile returning, "I actually feel tougher, stronger, because I feel moral when I'm with her. She brings out the best in me, Zack. She makes me want to be a better human being."

Zack swallowed hard. And at that very moment, he finally understood. Brianna Hudson was no here-today-gone-tomorrow airhead. Brianna Hudson may just turn out to be the love of his father's life.

Zack moved closer against his father, and Robert pulled him closer still. And they sat on the porch, father and son, and watched the cascade of land and beautiful mountain ranges for as far as the eye could see. For nearly an hour they sat out there, saying not a word, enjoying the home, the land Robert purchased nearly a decade ago. Until Robert, hearing something, looked away from the big picture of his property, and closer to home. "Who could that be?" he asked when he looked toward the entrance gate.

Zack looked too and saw a cab coming their way, the dust of the road kicking up behind it. When the cab stopped at the steps, and his mother, Sylvia Bellarouche, stepped out in her shades and all things Versace, he didn't know if he was elated or, given what his father had not an hour ago shared with him, disappointed.

"What in the world," Robert began to ask when he realized it was his ex., a woman he hadn't seen in nearly a year. He frowned. "What is she doing here?"

Zack stood up, feeling awkward. "Ma, hi," she said as Sylvia began walking up the steps.

"Get my luggage and pay the driver," Sylvia said to Zack, barking out orders the way he was accustomed. For some odd reason he always felt more uneasy with his mother than he ever felt with his father.

"Yes, ma'am," he said and hurried to do her bidding.

They kissed, cheek to cheek, as he passed by.

Sylvia then stood on the top step, looking at Robert. She wore a thin, flare dress and sandals and still had that same natural beauty that catapulted her into supermodel status when she was only nineteen. Robert had known and loved her for so long that he still couldn't resist admiring her beauty. By the way she removed her shades and gave him that impressive, metropolitan smile she had come to perfect, she knew it, too.

"Well, hello there, Mr. Colgate," she said to him.

"Hello yourself," he replied.

They stared into each other's eyes and Sylvia's face turned from whimsicalness to a mix of anxiety and concern. "Oh, Bobby," she said as she ran to him, kissed him on his lips and threw her arms around him.

Robert held her too. She was the mother of his beloved son and therefore would always have a special place in his heart. He held her tightly.

Zack, with his mother's luggage in tow and the cab driver in his cab and on his way, began heading up to the porch, careful not to drop anything and incur his mother's considerable wrath. But when he made it to the top step and saw his parents embracing, he stopped in his tracks. And for some strange reason, his heart didn't soar as he would have expected it to, but dropped, as if he suddenly realized that his father getting back with his mother wouldn't be such a great thing after all.

At that moment also Bree, still inside the house, came to the screen door. She had confirmed her airline reservation, packed most of her luggage, and was coming to let them know her flight schedule. However, when she saw Zack just standing there staring to the right of the door where she knew Robert was sitting, her heart dropped too. Had Robert fallen again? Had something happened to Robert again?

Bree snatched open the screen door and hurried out onto the porch, to make sure Robert didn't need her help. When she saw him sitting there, embracing some woman, who was now sitting on his lap and appeared to be sobbing, she, like Zack, stopped in her tracks too. And when Robert ran his hand through the woman's long, flowing blonde hair, and his eyes closed tighter, as if he was remembering her and how she felt in his arms, maybe even in his bed, Bree didn't think she could have felt more disappointed.

When Robert opened his eyes and saw Zack standing there, and then Bree, he immediately extricated Sylvia from his lap and stood both of them to their feet. "Brianna, hi," he said. "Were you able to book a flight?"

"Yes," Bree said, attempting to maintain her composure. *Never let them see you sweat, baby girl*, her father used to always tell her.

"Good," Robert said, pulling a handkerchief from his pocket and wiping his hands. He wore shorts and Bree could see where his penis was slightly engorged. The woman with him, although gently wiping her eyes, seemed to relish the scene. She even smiled through her tears.

"Brianna, come here," Robert suddenly ordered, his hand reaching out to clasp hers. Although Bree wasn't feeling this scene at all, she wasn't about to fly off the handle without knowing all of the facts. She walked over to him and allowed him to hold her hand. "I want you to meet Zack's mother, Sylvia Bellarouche. Sylvie, this is my lady, Brianna."

"Nice to meet you, Brianna," Sylvia said, extending her ultra-thin hand, smiling as if this was the best fun she'd had in a while.

"Brianna's a lawyer, Ma," Zack felt a need to say, as if Bree looked pathetic against his supermodel mother and needed some extra help. Why he felt the need to help her, however, was the amazing part to him.

"Oh, really?" Sylvia said. "A lawyer just like Bobby. How cute."

Since that didn't go over so well, Zack gave up and carried the luggage inside of the house.

"Have a seat, Sylvie," Robert ordered. Sylvia moved and sat in the seat where Zack had just vacated, the one directly next to Robert. Robert was about to move to correct Sylvia but Bree, not interested in playing games with this woman, removed her hand from his and sat in the chair across from them. Robert hesitated, he really wanted Bree, not Sylvia, beside him, but then he realized, as Bree had, that making an issue of it would only make it worse. He sat down.

"So how long have you two known each other?" Sylvia asked, her long legs crossed and her thin body leaned forward as she rubbed her calf. Her question was clearly directed to Bree, at whom she seemed unable to stop staring.

"Not long," Bree said.

"Oh, yes, that's right," Sylvia said. "You were one of his trainees at one point, weren't you?"

Like Zack, she had her spies at Colgate too, Bree realized. Then she nodded her head, just now understanding the full extent of the competition she faced. This witch was at first acting as if she'd never heard of Bree. Now Bree was convinced she not only had heard of her, but probably had a complete dossier on her. "That's right," Bree said.

"That's so unusual," Sylvia said. "Bobby has never dated the help. I mean not ever."

"Well he dated this help," Bree said, making it clear to Sylvia that she understood the game and would not be playing along. "Moved her into his house too, how about that?"

Robert smiled. Sylvia frowned. "That's hardly something to brag about."

"You mean the fact that we're shacking up?"

"That's exactly what I mean. Women of a certain class and status do not shack up, as you put it, with men."

"But you shacked up with Robert for over ten years. And kept coming back periodically for more and more," Bree couldn't resist adding.

This assertive response by Bree threw Sylvia. For some reason she was expecting a docile, Mississippi country bumpkin of a girl who would simply listen and learn. Bree, too, had an idea that Sylvia would be expecting docility too, and that was why she was pouncing.

"I did not shack up with Robert," Sylvia clarified, attempting to maintain her composure. "I had my own home that entire time."

"I have my own home too. Back in Dale, Mississippi. But I'm sure your spies told you that, too."

Robert laughed. "Isn't Brianna marvelous?" he said to his ex, causing her to look at him with daggers in her big, blue eyes. Then she caught herself, and smiled grandly.

"Oh, yes," she lied. "Marvy indeed."

"So how long are you planning on staying?" Bree asked Sylvia. She still had her issues with Robert and his hugging and, undoubtedly, kissing on the woman, but not in front of Miss Beauty Queen.

"I plan to stay as long as Bobby needs me."

"Then you can head back now, Sylvie," Robert said. "I'm fine."

Sylvia maintained her obvious fake smile. "You don't look so fine. You look underfed and under-cared for in every way. And I mean every way," she added as she moved a strand of Robert's hair from his face. Robert caught her hand.

"That's enough of that, all right?" he said to Sylvia, his grip tight. When he released her, she winced. But continued to smile. "Sure you don't want any of my home cooking?" she asked him.

"I'm positive," Robert said.

"He could use it," Bree said. "Zack's told me all about your world class recipes and since I've got a plane to catch," Bree added, rising to her feet, "you can stay here and cook for him. Cook until your heart's content. I'd better finish packing."

Robert could see the pain, the disappointment in her expressive brown eyes as she turned and headed back inside the house.

Sylvia smiled, feeling triumphant. "Well," she said. "Seems I came not a moment too soon. Who does that bitch think she is?"

"She's my woman," Robert said, standing, discarding his cane altogether. "And prayerfully, one day, my wife," he added, to Sylvia's shock.

And then he headed inside his home, in search of Brianna.

EIGHTEEN

Bree sat on the edge of the big, king-sized bed, tossing the last of her clothing into the suit case that sat on the luggage rack on the side of the bed. When the bedroom door opened, and Robert entered, closing the door behind him, she almost wanted to tell him to please leave her alone. She felt bad enough.

But Robert, instead, walked over to the bed and knelt down on his haunches in front of her, each of his hands on each one of her knees.

"When is your flight?" he asked her.

"At five thirty," Bree reluctantly said. But Robert, this close to her, always made her feel heady, trapped even, but in a wonderful way.

His blue eyes stared into her brown ones, and his pain was as searing as hers.

"I care about Sylvie," he said, as he began to unbutton Bree's jeans. "She's Zack's mother. I will always care about Sylvie," he added, as he unzipped her jeans. "But I love you." He pulled her jeans and panties all the way down to her ankles, and then off altogether, and then he pulled her into his arms. Her legs wrapped around him as he held her, his body pressed hard against her now bare womanhood. Then his lips pressed lightly and then roughly onto hers as he began kissing her in circular, lovemaking-in-and-of -itself kissing that made her feel immediately drunk by the fantastic taste of him, and she wrapped her arms around him, too.

When they stopped kissing, tears appeared in her eyes. They leaned forehead to forehead against each other as he removed his jersey from over his head and began unbuttoning her blouse.

"You shouldn't have let her sit on your lap," Bree admonished.

"I know, sweetheart. I hadn't seen her in a long time and it just happened."

"You rubbed her hair. You were remembering her. Weren't you?"

Robert stopped unbuttoning and looked at Bree. "I don't love her that way, Brianna. I care deeply about her. But I am not in love with her. And I wouldn't trust her as far as I can blow her away from me."

Bree smiled. "She's very beautiful."

Robert began unbuttoning her blouse again. "If you go for that sort of thing, yes, she is."

Bree playfully hit him upside his head. "You went for that sort of thing for over a decade, buddy, don't forget that."

"Yes, I did," Robert said, opening her blouse and lifting her bra up. "Then a decade later I met you and realized the error of my ways."

Bree smiled. But as Robert stared at her now exposed breasts, her smile began to leave. The way he stared at her, and the fact that they had not had sex in over two months, since his accident, removed all levity. This was sensual business now. Because Robert's look made Bree's body began to tremble, made her want him inside of her this very instant.

But Robert didn't roll like that. No way was he going to see this wonderful body and not possess every inch of it. He kissed her breasts, he always had to start there, his mouth teasing her nipples. But that wasn't what he was craving. He moved down her body, slowly and sensually, until he arrived at his destination. And he ate it up, kissing all around it and then licking her with expert licks. He loved the scent of her, the beauty of being with her, that he kissed and licked and sucked her so long, and then longer and longer, getting rougher and rougher until she was wiggling her body to break free, and not to break free, in a tug of war that made her feel more desirable than even the most desirable of supermodels could have felt. Right here and right now Robert wanted her above any other woman, and she could feel his want.

He could feel it too, as his mouth seemed seared onto her pussy, as she splattered her wetness all over his mouth and made him so hungry for her that he thought he'd lose it if he didn't get inside of her and get inside of her right away.

He removed his shorts, pulled her further on the bed, and got inside of her, sliding his massive rod into her with a purpose that seemed beyond carnal. He loved this woman and wanted to show it. And he did, as he entered her, as he wrapped her in his arms and gyrated all over her.

Outside, on the porch, Zack was leaned against the rail while his mother angrily paced the floor.

"Marry her?" she said. "Is he out of his mind? Marry her. He's known me for over twenty years and never once had he asked me to marry him. Never once. Now he was considering making her his bride? *Her*? Some nigger witch from *Mississippi*? Are you fucking kidding me?"

"He loves her, Ma," Zack said but his mother rounded on him with a look that melted his eyes.

"You shut up! Dropped out of school again."

"To help Dad."

"Your Dad doesn't need your help. Doesn't need mine either. He's got his African queen now, his Mississippi southern belle now. He doesn't need either one of us." Then she stopped pacing, her arms folded. "How could he, Zack? He wants to marry *her*? Why didn't he do this when I was in the bloom of my years? Why didn't he marry some young, beautiful girl when I was still young and beautiful too?"

"You are still beautiful," Zack said.

"But I'm not young anymore. And I never will be." Then she dismissed the sentiment, became hard again. Began pacing again. "And a nigger to boot," she said. "And not a rich, sophisticated one, oh no, that would be too understandable. But to go and dredge up some poor bitch who wouldn't know the Sorbonne in Paris from a rib joint in Jersey? That father of yours, I declare. He's always had a mind of his own and man is he using it now. But to upstage me? Nobody upstages me," Sylvia said with certainty and then hesitated. And before Zack knew anything she was moving fast for the screen door, and then moving even faster into the house.

She first tried the kitchen for some reason, and then, realizing the witch did mention packing, headed for the master bedroom of a home she knew so well. When she made her way down the long hall to the bedroom at the end of it, she was disappointed to see that the door was closed. But she heard the noise before she even made it all the way up to the door.

They were fucking, pure and simple. Sylvia knew it when she heard it. There was the bed shaking and the moaning. She remembered how wonderful Robert used to feel inside of her, how even after they had broken up she would travel many miles back to Chicago just for him to fuck her again. And she did this repeatedly and did it for years after. No man, not to this day, had ever made her feel the way that big, thick iron rod of

Robert's made her feel. And she was ready to sling open that bedroom door and put an end to Brianna achieving that feeling.

But then she heard an oddity. Robert started moaning too. In all of her previous years with him, he never used to make a sound. He, in fact, seemed to take some twisted pleasure, some twisted sense of power in hearing her make all of the noise. But now he was moaning and groaning as if this woman was in control, not him, as if she had the power. And this little oddity stopped Sylvia in her tracks. Was it true, she wondered. Had Robert Colgate, Mr. Confirmed Bachelor, actually and truly fallen head over heels? *Robert*? Her heart fell through her shoe.

The meeting wasn't held at Colgate and Associates, but at Alan DeFrame's new home, Lawrence and Lowe law firm, in the Chicago suburbs. Bree and Lee Clayton were escorted to the conference room where they found themselves waiting for far longer than the respectable few minutes. Which didn't surprise Bree in the least. She had yet to meet a man tackier than Alan DeFrame.

Besides her mind was back in Wyoming. She stood at the window in the conference room, overlooking a dreary Chicago morning, and remembered how passionately Robert made love to her before she left. And afterwards, while he was still lingering inside of her, while he was still lying on top of her, he looked at her with such a loving expression that it still gave her goose bumps.

"You're my lady, Brianna," he had said. "There's no other woman anywhere on the face of this earth that I want, or need, more than you. You're my lady. You. And don't you ever forget that, you understand me?"

Bree could do nothing but lay there and nod, her heart filled with love for him, her eyes fighting back tears as he continued to stare deep into them. And, remarkable, given his weakened state, his manhood began to expand once more, and his gyrating slowly, but surely, began again.

"But Robert," Bree said with a smile, "you'll overexert yourself if we do it again."

Robert smiled too, kissed her on the forehead. "Oh, my sweet thing," he said, his movements increasing, "there's no way making love to you could ever be an overexertion. Just relax," he said as he lay further down on her, holding her tightly against him, his penis moving in and out with such a sensual slide that it started making her drowsy. "Relax and let me enjoy every solitary inch of you again."

"Bree," Lee Clayton said, apparently for the second time, and Bree quickly turned from her daydreams at the large window. Alan and Deidra Dentry were sitting at the conference table. "They're ready," Lee proclaimed.

Bree hurried to the table and sat, once again, beside Lee. She opened a large file she had in front of her.

"First of all," Alan said, pushing his glasses on his face, looking as smug as Bree remembered him, "we are not interested in any settlement offer." Bree glanced at Deidra. She was smiling, enjoying her newfound fame as the accuser of a powerhouse like Robert Colgate. "We feel we have the kind of evidence, the kind of case that must have its day in court."

"Oh, really now," Bree said. "And what evidence is that? All we've heard so far is her word against Mr. Colgate's."

"And that's all I'll need, believe that," Deidra said. "No jury of my peers is going to disbelieve anything I say."

"It's actually a jury of Mr. Colgate's peers that will be trying to case, but that's neither here or there. That simply goes to your incompetence as an attorney, not to this matter before us."

"You bitch!" Deidra fumed. "How dare you call me incompetent!"

Alan pat Deidra on the hand. It did work to calm her back down.

"Here's the deal," Bree said, uninterested in spending any more time with those two than was necessary. "You either drop this lawsuit or we will go public."

Deidra frowned. "Go public? It's already public, you idiot!"

"What are you referencing, Bree?" Alan asked her.

"If you, Deidra, decide to continue this charade of yours--"

"It's not a charade! He did harass me!"

"Yeah, right," Bree said, "you give it up to Alan, you give it up to Bret Drysdale, you give it up to anybody and everybody who asked you for some. But for Mr. Colgate, for the head man himself, he has to harass you to get a piece? You must take us for fools!"

"Keep talking," Deidra said, angry, "and I'll suit you for slander as quick as you can say 'I's sorry.'"

Bree looked at Deidra as if she had lost her mind. *I's sorry*? What the hell kind of English is that?"

"My schedule is tight, ladies," Alan said. "Let's get on with it, shall we?"

"Yes, lets," Alan said. "My schedule is tight also. So again, Bree, what's this grand deal you're here to offer us?"

"Drop this idiotic lawsuit, or prepare for the onslaught."

Alan frowned. "What onslaught?"

"We will make public every family secret the Dentry family has held from generations back, and we will do so repeatedly."

Deidra smiled. "What are you talking about? What family secrets?"

"Oh, we've got a ton. From illegitimate black babies, to alcoholism, insanity, assaults, rapes, and, as for that wonderful former Supreme Court Justice granddaddy of yours, the second family in Virginia and the physical abuse of the first family."

Deidra's' smile was now gone. She stared at Bree. "How did you. . . How could you know . . ." She looked at Alan.

Alan, at first, had planned to dismiss such talk. Go public all you want, he had planned to say. But that look on Deidra's face stopped him cold.

"And we won't stop there," Lee said. "Because there is that matter of an abortion, by you, Miss Dentry, because the father, to our shock, happens to be your father's best friend."

Deidra touched Alan's shirtsleeve, her face unable to conceal her growing terror. Alan looked at Deidra.

"It's nothing but talk," he said to her, confused by her reaction. "I can't, we can't--"

"Yes, we can allow it," Alan assured her. "It's just a bunch of smoke and mirrors anyway, a bunch of innuendo and gossip and a lot of nothing in the end. Let'em go public. Who cares?"

"No!" Deidra shouted. "It'll destroy my mother, my family. No!" She looked at Bree. "You will not publish any of that craziness, I mean none of it."

"Drop your lawsuit, apologize to Mr. Colgate, admit you lied and lied repeatedly on him, and you have nothing to worry about. But if you choose to fight, if you chose to continue this nonsense, then fine. Continue it. Fight on. But rest assured we will be fighting back and fighting back with everything we can find, every nasty little rumor we can dig up. Because if you think for a second, Deidra, that I'll sit back and let you destroy the reputation of the most honest, the most forthright man I have ever met, then you are monumentally misinformed."

Deidra stared at Bree with such fire in her eyes that Bree wondered if she would singe herself. Then she stood and left the room. Alan stood too, still confused, and followed her, telling them to hold on a moment as he went.

When the door closed, Lee smiled. "It worked," he said. "I can't believe it worked."

"I told you it would," Bree said. "Deidra is the most prideful woman in the world. If these rumors or whatever you want to call them, become public knowledge, because water cooler conversations, she would be doomed. And so would that Dentry legacy they have always worked so hard to achieve."

"Then why in hell did she bring this lawsuit to begin with?"

Bree smiled. "Pure vengeance," she said. "She lost the spot and therefore the man who selected Pru Cameron instead of her must be punished. It's a family tradition with the Dentrys. That's what my research found, and I was amazed at how obvious the pattern was."

"And so she goes to Alan, who had gotten fired--"

"And who had undoubtedly promised her the position for sleeping with him," Bree added, "yes, she went to Alan."

"And Alan wouldn't mind a little revenge of his own for Colgate firing him."

"Exactly," Bree said. "It was payback for both of them. And payback is a bitch, it really is, but it's a bitch that bites both ways."

Lee smiled, and then laughed. "If I get in trouble," he said, "I want you as my attorney."

Bree laughed. As she did, however, the door opened again, and Alan reemerged, only this time he was alone.

He stood at the table in front of them. "Against my advice, completely against it, my client has decided to agree to your terms."

Bree's heart soared.

"But as for me," Alan said, "I'll keep that story as alive as if it was the very air people breathe. Robert Colgate will never be free of those allegations."

"Even though they're a pack of lies?" Bree asked.

"Especially so," Alan, true to himself through and through, said.

Bree nodded. "Okay," she said, reached into her briefcase, pulled out her small recorder, and pressed play.

"You know why," Alan was recorded saying, *"because, contrary to what you may think, Mr. Colgate has put me solely in charge of the selection process. It's one hundred percent my decision. However, I will decide in your favor, Bree, and decide without hesitation, if you give me what I want."*

"And what exactly is that?" Bree was recorded asking.

"Ah come on, Brianna! The airhead act doesn't do you justice and I'm way too smart to fall for it. You know what I want. You know I've wanted it since the moment I laid eyes on you. I want to fuck you, that's what I want."

"Aren't Pru and Deidra and those other pretty Prada girls giving you that already?"

"Pru, are you kidding? Who the hell wants that prudish bitch?"

"Deidra then, surely."

"Oh, yes, Deidra is available to me anytime I want her. Only that kind of easy lay takes the excitement out of it, know what I'm saying? So forget about her. If you give me what I want, you're in. No ands, ifs or buts about it. You're in."

"I want in," Bree was recorded saying, *"but never like that."*

Bree pressed the stop button and looked at Alan. He stared at her, his smug arrogance now replaced with uncertain fear.

"What do you want us to do?" he asked.

NINETEEN

Zack came into the kitchen to find his mother staring out of the window. Her bags were packed and ready to go. She, in fact, would have left last night but she hoped to give it another try with Robert after Bree left town. She even crept to his bedroom naked late that night, hoping to surprise him enough that he'd forget Bree and give her some. But he had locked his bedroom door.

Zack had heard her crept, too, and had heard her bang on his father's bedroom door in anger when she realized it was locked, and then she gave up and went to bed. It was a painful night, Zack recalled. And the pain continued when he glanced out of the kitchen window and saw his father working out on a bench press in shorts and a sleeveless shirt, and realized that was who his mother was standing there staring at, he sighed. And in sighing, got his mother's attention.

"Where were you all morning?" she asked him.

"Running some errands for Dad," he replied. "He's back there, right?' he asked, as if he didn't know already.

"Yes,' Sylvia said, turning back to look out of the window, "looking as fit as ever. It's amazing that a man like him had a high attack two months ago." Especially yesterday, she thought inwardly, with that workout he put on that Brianna person.

"Yeah," Zack said, walking up to the window and looking out too. "I'm built nothing like him."

Sylvia glanced at her son, and then back at Robert. "No."

"It's probably only natural though," Zack said. "Since he's not my father."

Sylvia stopped cold, and then turned at looked at Zack. "What did you say?" she asked him, her face a mask of anguish.

"I've known for years," Zack said, still staring at Robert working out. "He's not my father." Then he looked at Sylvia. "Is he?"

Sylvia, looking stricken, hurried to the door and yelled for Robert. "Robert, please come," she yelled. "Please come now!"

Robert, not used to Sylvia showing that kind of emotion, hurried from his bench press and ran across the back patio and into the house. When he arrived in the kitchen, his face drenched in the sweat that his best workout in months created, he saw Sylvia standing beside Zack.

"What is it, what's wrong?" he asked. But Sylvia was staring at Zack, and Zack was staring at her.

"How did you know?" she asked Zack.

"It bothered me for years, but I didn't know how to ask. So I just kept looking. You'd drop hints every now and then, but that wasn't what did it for me, not really."

"What did it for you then?"

"A gut feeling. I just knew he wasn't my biological father, I just knew it. We were nothing alike. We looked nothing alike. I just knew it. But I couldn't figure out the other part."

Sylvia frowned. "What other part?"

"Why Dad would keep having me around? Why he never treated me like anything but the son he loved. I mean, he loves me more than you do, everybody knows that, and you're my biological mother. And I was looking for signs of mistreatment, too. Boy, did I look. But they were never there. He just kept loving me. That's why I always wanted to be around him, and used to beg you to let me live with him after y'all broke up. Because he loved me so much, and I didn't want to lose that."

"But if you knew," Sylvia said, "why did you keep trying to get us back together, if you knew Robert wasn't your real father?"

"Fear," Zack said and Robert's heart went out to him, understanding exactly what he meant.

But Sylvia didn't understand it at all. "Fear?" she asked. "Fear of what?"

"Of him not wanting me around anymore, if there was no chance of getting you back."

"But," Sylvia started, still not understanding. "But that can't be right. That can't be the only reason you wanted us back together."

"But it was. I knew you weren't good for him. I love you, Mom, but you were terrible for Dad. I just had to keep him interested in you as his potential wife, so that he could stay interested in me as his potential son. Or, at least, stepson if he married you. That would at least give me some claim to him."

Robert's heart dropped. It was all true. Sylvia admitted it, in a fit of rage, when Zack was only two years old. The father, according to her, could be anybody. She was on location in Greece for months, was drunk and doped up most of that time, and she slept around liberally, at least that was how she had put it.

Robert walked up to Zack and put his hands on either one of his small shoulders. "You're right, Zackary," he said. "I'm not your biological father. But you are my son. You're nobody else's but mine. You understand me?"

Zack's heart soared, as tears appeared in his eyes. "Yes, sir," he said to the man he loved more than life itself. And he threw himself in his father's arms.

Robert wrapped his arms around Zack. This was his boy, his only child, even though they shared no blood kinship. But this was his child and would always be his child. He looked at Sylvia. And he could see the regret, the pain of her trail of bad decisions, deep within her eyes. She wanted him to hold her. Her eyes were begging him to hold her. But Robert, instead, took his son and walked back out of the kitchen door.

Three hours later, after lunch, and Robert was in that same kitchen washing dishes, when Zack yelled: "Dad, come here!"

"What is it, Zack?" Robert asked, relieved that Sylvia and her drama had packed up and left, and not interested in any more.

"Just get in here," Zack replied. "It's about you."

Robert frowned, set the plate he was washing in the drain, and walked into his living room, drying his hands on a towel as he came. "About me?" he asked.

"Yeah," Zack said, staring at the TV. Robert walked up to the back of the sofa where Zack sat, and stared at the TV, too.

It was an apparent press conference and Bree, to Robert's surprised, was there. Also present was Lee Clayton, Alan DeFrame, and Deidra Dentry. "What's this about?" he asked.

"Has to be about you," Zack said. "Or Alan and that Deidra woman wouldn't be there. And hey Dad, that's probably why Lee Clayton was helping Bree. He was helping her to clear your name."

Robert stared at Bree, at the most gorgeous woman in the world to him. His love for her couldn't possibly be any stronger.

"My client has a brief statement," Alan stood behind the podium and said. "After which there will be no questions or no further comments on this matter." Then he stepped aside and allowed Deidra to step forward.

"I just want to say," she read from her prepared remarks, "that I have decided to drop my lawsuit against Robert Colgate." The camera clicks went wild. She hesitated, glanced at Bree, but continued. "After searching my conscience and reviewing in my mind the events of the past months, I reached the conclusion that I have made a dreadful mistake. Mr. Colgate wasn't the man who was harassing me. In fact, no one at Colgate and Associates was harassing me. It was just a terrible misunderstanding on my part. I therefore contacted his attorneys," she looked back at Bree and Lee, neither of which were Robert's attorneys of record, "and we all agreed that I should come forward with the truth. So therefore I wish to cancel any lawsuit and to apologize to Mr. Colgate and his family for all of the pain that my allegations had undoubtedly caused them. Thank-you."

And she and Alan, and Bree and Lee walked off of the stage united.

Zack looked back at his father. "Wow," he said. "You think Bree orchestrated that?"

Robert smiled. "It would be just like her," he said with a grin. Wow, he thought, was right.

The revolving doors of Colgate and Associates revolved to the entrance as Robert entered the lobby and headed for the elevators. It had been over two months since he last stepped foot in his building, and he felt like he was coming back home. Monty had met the company plane and entered the building with him. The two men made their way to the tower.

But first Robert stopped the elevator on the twenty-first floor, stepped off, told Monty he'd see him in a few, and made his way to Brianna's office.

Her secretary, stunned to see Robert, nearly swallowed her chewing gum. And then she stood to her feet.

"Mr. Colgate," she said.

"Hello, Alice," he said without breaking his stride. "Miss Hudson in?"

"No, sir," Alice said to Robert's disappointment. He had wanted to surprise her.

He stopped walking.

"At least not in her office. She's in Mr. Dougan's office up in the tower, from what I understand, sir."

Robert hesitated. Dougan. It figures, he thought. "Thanks, Alice," he said, and then headed in Dougan's direction.

Bree was already there. Being drilled, schooled, scolded, all of the above, by Matt and Wade Furst.

"It's bad enough," Matt said, "to not even know that you had even met with my client's accusers, but to then hold a joint press conference with them and not even bother to mention it to me? The attorney of record? It's downright criminal, I tell you!"

"And you're the one who fired Pru Cameron for insubordination," Wade reminded her. "Yet nothing Pru has ever done could ever match your little stunt."

"And that's exactly what it is," Matt added. "A stunt. Where the hell do you get off?" he wanted to know.

His office door opened and Robert, with Matt's secretary behind him trying to give Matt warning, walked in.

Matt and Wade both flew to their feet. Bree, who was already standing, smiled.

"Well, hello there," she said.

"May I join the inquisition?" Robert asked, smiling too.

Bree laughed.

"It's hardly funny, Bobby," Matt said. "And what are you doing here? We weren't expecting you back for another week. But I guess that's another thing Bree failed to mention."

"Bree didn't know herself," Robert said. He wanted to pull her in his arms, but knew such a display of affection would do her no favors in this room. But he did give her a good look over. "What's going on here?" he asked her.

"You said it right," Bree said. "An inquisition."

"That's not fair," Matt said, "and you know it. Did you know about this, Bobby? This joint press conference she held?"

"No, I didn't. I was washing dishes, minding my own business, when my son called me to the television."

"Did Zack come with you?" Bree wanted to know.

"No. I told him we should be back sometime tomorrow."

Bree smiled. "Good."

"I thought we'd first go pick up your younger siblings, let them join us for a few days in Laramie."

"Oh, Robert, that would be great!"

He also had to tell her about the fact that Zack wasn't his biological son, and how Zack's knowledge of it didn't change their close father/son relationship one iota, and he didn't want her knowledge of it to change anything either. But that would be a very private conversation.

"So you didn't know, either," Matt said. "You were as shocked as the rest of us. What the hell is going on here, Bobby? I didn't give Hudson or Lee Clayton any right to represent you at any meeting! Let alone calling some joint press conference. What the hell kind of mutiny is this?"

"Keep your shirt on, Matt, it's over with," Robert said.

"But where does she get off?"

"She gets off with me," Robert said. "That's where she gets off. Anything that concerns me is her business and her purview. She was just exercising her right."

Matt exhaled. "It's a damnable thing, I'll tell you that, Bobby. A damnable thing."

"Don't you think you're missing the point," Bree said. "Isn't the fact that Deidra finally came clean the real point here?"

Matt ran his hand through his gray hair. "Of course it is. But the way you went about it, young lady, was wrong. Pure and simple. And if you weren't who you are, I would have fired you on the spot, or at least forced your resignation."

"I had to keep the circle small," Bree explained. "I didn't want any glitches, not until I had that witch on TV retracting her nonsense. Now that that's done, yes, Mr. Dougan, you're right. I went about it all wrong. And I should be forced to resign, or fired." She looked at Robert. "That's why my resignation is already on your desk."

Robert stared at her.

"You and I working together isn't going to work," she said with a smile. "I think I need to chart my own course, at least for now."

"Good decision," Wade said, but the only opinion that mattered to Bree was Robert's.

But he wasn't giving an opinion. "Let's go, I need to talk to you." He looked at Matt and Wade. "We'll talk later," he warned.

Outside of Matt's office and Robert and Bree headed around the corridor on the top floor to Robert's suite of offices. After speaking to the tower staff, they made their way into his office. As soon as the door closed, he pinned Bree against it.

"I'm going to have to decline your resignation," he said as he gave her small kisses on her lips.

"Decline it? But why?"

"It won't work otherwise."

"What won't work?"

Robert stared into her eyes. "The new name."

Bree was lost. "Robert, what are you talking about?"

"I'm changing the name of Colgate and Associates. The new name will be Colgate and Colgate, to accommodate my new wife and law partner."

Bree's heart began to pound. "Your new wife?"

Robert smiled. "If you'll marry me, yes, Brianna. My new wife. Will you become my wife?"

Bree was speechless. She just stood there, staring at Robert.

Robert's heart now began to pound. When she still didn't accept, or say anything, he became scared.

"You're giving me a heart attack here, Brianna, please say yes."

And she breathe again. And smiled. "Yes," she said like an exhale. "I'll be thrilled to be your wife."

And my law partner?" he asked.

"That'll be a little trickier, but yes. And your partner."

It was Robert's time to be speechless, as he couldn't believe how blessed he was. But instead of finding his voice, he found Bree's mouth and gave her a kiss that shook them both, and took their breath away.

ABOUT THE AUTHOR

Katherine Cachitorie is the bestselling author of several novels, including Some Came Desperate: A Love Saga and When We Get Married.

Made in the USA
Lexington, KY
22 November 2011